Legendary players, major events and a history and tradition to stand shoulder to shoulder with the best.

Preston North End has been alive and kicking for more than 110 years, around to help celebrate no fewer than six of the famous town pageants which occur only once every twenty years. Preston Guilds.

This publication is a pictorial history of a famous football club, presented to allow the pictures to help the words to unveil the story.

It randomly captures the spirit through the eras - the Invincibles of late last century, the glorious Tom Finney golden days of the 50's right through to the present day.

Two dozen or so of the great characters and the great occasions are included; some glories recalled and some disappointments remembered.

This is no … sporting hist … There are det… analyses as you would expect, but, for the most part, this is an easy-read aimed to entertain as much as to inform.

Football has always been close to the very hearts of the people of Lancashire, a traditional hotbed for the national game. And nowhere in the county have passions run stronger than in the town of Preston.

All supporters and followers will have their own favourite players and games and events that stand out for one reason or another.

This is an attempt to draw on the memory bank and place on permanent record just some of the men and the matches contributing to a stunning history of a very special football club - Preston North End.

SHANKLY

Bill Shankly O.B.E. was a man respected highly on Merseyside, (or should it be idolised), for his managerial achievements with Liverpool F.C. over a 15 year period. But the same enthusiastic character spent an even longer spell at Deepdale - as a player.

He signed for P.N.E. in July 1933 from Carlisle Utd. having previously been with Glenbuck Cherrypickers.

Standing 5'7" tall Bill was a fitness fanatic bursting with energy and full of self-confidence. In his first season with Preston he helped the club to promotion back to Division One with some gritty displays as an attacking wing-half.

He played in what was a very good era for the club appearing in two successive F.A. Cup Finals at Wembley. Although he received a losers medal in 1937 he gained his coveted winners medal the following year when George Mutch's goal decided the game.

His fierce tenacity and knowledge of the game caught the eye of the Scottish International selectors and he went on to win five full caps.

Bill was one of the players whose careers (and lives) were interrupted by the war. He still played for P.N.E whenever possible during the war and was still playing first team football in 1949 before stepping down to become player/coach to our Reserves.

Ten years and a few clubs later he landed at Liverpool - the rest is history.

A handsome young Bill Shankly in his early days at P.N.E. He went on to become one of the most influential characters in the game.

Fred Else. One of the many outstanding North End keepers.

Bobby Ham

Something to chew on. P.N.E. have had players with surnames such as HAM, VEALL, LAMB and MUSTARD.

Gary Swann

Ex-North Ender's surnames when paired with others can give some unusual combinations;
BRIGHT - SPARK,
CRAVEN - DICKIE,
BIRD - SWANN,
ORR - ELSE - WATT,
ROY - RODGERS,
TICKLE - PINCH,
BAKER - COOK - BARBER,
TWIST - DAGGER,
TEMPLE - CROSS,
BELL - PEEL,
CRANSTON - BRANSTON
HANNIGAN - BRANAGAN

David Brown

North End have some colourful characters in the past, namely Ellis GREEN, Frank WHITE, David BROWN, and Terry GRAY.

Two former P.N.E. keepers have been Fred FOX and George WOLF.

<u>THE GAME OF THE NAME</u>

BLACK PRINCE

Preston North End once boasted a centre forward they signed for £20,000 and later sold for £15,000. During the six seasons in between he scored 114 goals in 197 matches..not a bad value-for-money deal at £5,000!

His name - Alex Dawson; his business - scoring goals.

Christened the "Black Prince" he will go down in the Deepdale annals as an undisputed hero. Not as the most skillful player ever to rub Dubbin in his boots, but as a goalscorer second to none.

His goals per game record could only be compared to that of Charlie Wayman.

Born in Scotland, Dawson signed for Manchester United at fifteen and had five seasons there before moving to Preston. He later had spells with Bury, Brighton, and Brentford before drifting into the non-Leaugue with Corby.

His goals in games records reads: Manchester United 45 in 80, P.N.E. 114 in 197, Bury 21 in 49, Brighton 26 in 53 and Brentford 6 in 10. He retired from the full-time scene in 1970, 15 years after his debut.

Dawson - feared by goalkeepers and centre-halves alike.

Dawson scored on his P.N.E. debut, at Rotherham, and also found the net on his biggest day in football, in the 1964 F.A. Cup Final when P.N.E. lost to West Ham.

After football he moved to Kettering working for a plastics company and in the early '80s had a successful hip replacement operation.

PRESTON UNITED

Two ex-North End players have been manager of Manchester United. Tommy Docherty and Frank O'Farrell. They are pictured in the 1959 P.N.E. line up where they both played as half backs. (O'Farrell standing extreme right, and Docherty standing extreme left.)

Three ex-United players have been manager of Preston North End - Bobby Charlton, Nobby Stiles and Brian Kidd. Charlton and Stiles, of course, ex-England World Cup winners in '66.

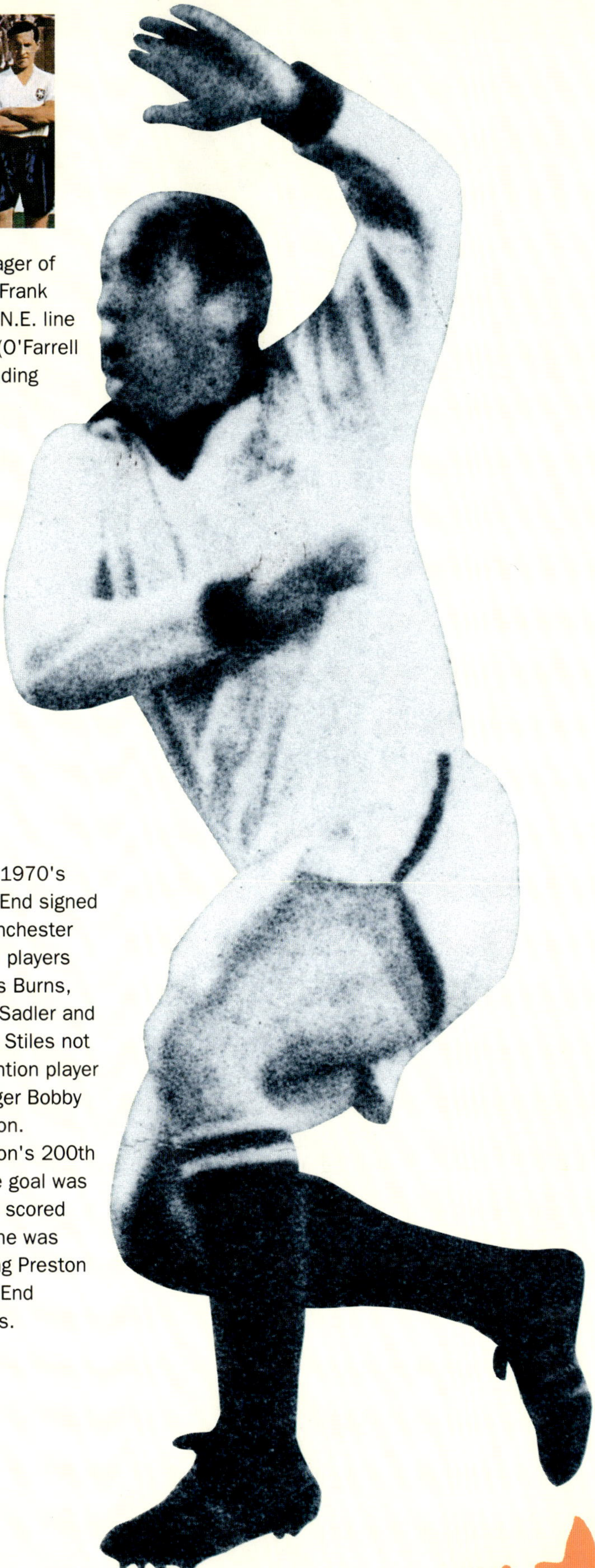

In the 1970's North End signed ex-Manchester United players Francis Burns, David Sadler and Nobby Stiles not to mention player manager Bobby Charlton. Charlton's 200th league goal was in fact scored while he was wearing Preston North End colours.

One of North End's most inspiring post-war captains was former United man Nobby Lawton. He led out the P.N.E. 1964 Cup Final team which included another ex-Red, Alex Dawson.

During the war North End played a home game against Manchester United at Leyland Motors ground, P.N.E. won 3-1. Deepdale was closed down.

After the war North End played a 6th round F.A. cup tie against United at Manchester City's ground. In the previous round P.N.E. had beat City, also at Maine Road. Old Trafford was shut down.

Manchester United used to be called Newton Heath. Their first season with the new name was the 1902/03 season. They played P.N.E. in a Preston Guild Week friendly 5 days before that season started so it is quite likely that their first game under the new Manchester United name was at Deepdale. P.N.E. won 5-1.

Back Row L/R: R. Holmes, N.J. Ross, D. Russel, R. Howarth, J. Graham, R.H. Mills-Roberts.
Front Row L/R: J. Gordon, J.Ross, J. Goodall, F. Dewhurst, G. Drummond.

The Invincibles

Preston North End has a history and a tradition second to none. The first winners of the Football League (1888-89, when they also won the F.A. Cup) and Football League champions the following season - not bad for starters....

Position	The Football League 1888 · 1889 (Alphabetically Arranged.)	Accrington	Aston Villa	B'burn Rovers	Blt'n Wanderers	Burnley	Derby County	Everton	Notts County	Preston N.E	Stoke	West Brom. Albion	W'hampton Wanderers	Won	Lost	Drawn		For	Against	Points	Position
		Results of 132 Matches												No. of Matches 22 Each				Goals			
7	Accrington	.. ..	34 11	55 02	14 23	51 22	11 62	12 31	33 12	00 02	42 20	22 21	44 04	6	8	8		48	48	20	7
2	Aston Villa	43 11	.. ..	61 15	32 62	42 04	42 25	21 02	91 42	11 02	51 11	20 33	11 21	12	5	5		61	43	29	2
4	B'burn Rovers	55 20	16 51	.. ..	44 23	71 42	20 30	30 13	33 52	01 22	52 12	62 12	22 22	10	6	6		66	45	26	4
5	Blt'n Wanderers	41 32	23 26	44 32	.. ..	34 14	36 32	62 12	40 73	18 25	21 22	51 12	23 21	10	10	2		63	59	22	5
9	Burnley	15 22	24 40	17 24	43 41	.. ..	10 01	22 23	16 10	25 22	34 21	34 20	14 04	7	12	3	·	42	62	17	9
10	Derby County	11 26	24 52	02 03	63 23	01 10	.. ..	24 26	32 52	23 05	21 11	12 05	14 30	7	13	2		41	60	16	10
8	Everton	21 13	12 20	03 31	26 21	22 32	42 62	.. ..	21 12	03 02	00 21	14 01	05 12	9	11	2		35	47	20	8
11	Notts County	33 21	19 24	33 25	04 37	61 01	23 25	12 31	.. ..	07 14	03 03	24 21	30 12	5	15	2		39	73	12	11
1	Preston N.E	00 20	71 24	10 22	31 52	52 22	32 50	30 20	70 41	.. ..	70 30	30 50	40 52	18	·	4		74	15	40	1
12	Stoke	24 02	15 11	25 21	12 22	43 12	12 11	00 12	30 30	07 03	.. ..	02 02	01 14	4	14	4		26	51	12	12
6	West Brom. Albion	22 12	02 33	26 21	15 21	43 02	21 50	41 10	42 12	03 05	20 20	.. ..	12 13	10	10	2		40	46	22	6
3	Wolverhampton Wanderers	44 40	11 12	22 22	32 12	41 40	41 03	50 21	03 21	04 25	10 41	21 31	.. ..	12	6	4		57	37	28	3
	Goals For	48	61	66	63	42	41	35	39	74	26	40	51	110	110	44		586	586	264	
	Goals against	48	43	45	59	62	60	47	73	15	51	46	37	April 1889. A.H. Richards.							

(1) North End. (2) Aston Villa (3) Wolverh'tn Wand. (4) B'burn Rovers (5) Bolton Wand (6) West Brom. (7) Accrington (8) Everton (9) Burnley (10) Derby Cty (11) Notts Cty (12) Stoke.

Hand written copy of League results season 1888-1889 from the Football League Minute Book.

And little wonder that the supreme success stories of the period earned the club the proud nickname of The Invincibles.

One William Sudell was at the heart of things from the word go. A local mill worker, Sudell played in the first North End game under Association rules against Eagley. Sudell campaigned to have professionalism legalised and was a major football figure of his day.

The incredible success Sudell brought to Deepdale is best illustrated through the help of statistical references.

Between August 22nd 1885 and April 1886 North End were undefeated winning 59 of their 64 matches and scoring 318 goals while conceding only 60.

Another feat worthy of note comes from the fact that in 1887-88 P.N.E. won 42 consecutive matches; the following season the club became one of the founder members of the Football League.

A limited company was formed in 1893 which marked the end of the Sudell reign, but the genius of the man remained fully recognised. Under Sudell P.N.E. truly were The Invincibles, served so well by many great players, Ross and Goodall to name but two.

The envy of the club's achievements spread far and wide. Everton looked for direction from the goings on at Deepdale and enticed the talented Ross with a staggering offer of £10 a month.

The inspirational Scot was a favourite son at Preston, but his departure caused few tears to shed - it simply allowed a gap in the team for a recruit from the ever-increasing number of young players.

Preston North End were "the" team of the moment, the club used as a yard stick throughout the land.

William Sudell - associated with Preston North End for 28 years.

THE COWBOY

Any of today's footballers who consider themselves tough could do worse than to have a chat with a real soccer hard man - Willie Cunningham. For starters, Willie combined the first six years as a player with working down the pit!

Willie joined P.N.E in the July of 1949 - he became an institution, nicknamed "The Cowboy".

He played hundreds of games down at Deepdale, represented his beloved Scotland at international level, turned out in a World Cup and took part in an F.A. Cup Final - not bad for a pit boy from the tiny North of the Border village of Hill'obeth.

But Willie Cunningham's story is by no means a Roy of the Rovers classic. Whatever the wee man with the big heart has got out of life he has grafted for it.

Born in Fife in 1925 he came through his local school ranks with a certain Jimmy Baxter, his cousin, who also went on to play in the same North End team.

Then a centre-half he was invited to join Dunfermline as a £3-a-week part-timer. He was eighteen then but had already been working down the mines for four years.

Life was far from easy for the young Cunningham and he continued to combine mining with soccer until he was 24 and playing at Airdrie.

A £5,000 fee brought him south of the border to Deepdale and he stayed a fixture in the team until 1963 playing 440 league games in 13 seasons.

On retirement he had a short spell as a player-manager with Southport before returning to Deepdale as a reserve team trainer.

**Willie Cunningham-
great player,
great character.**

SINGLE MINDED DOUBLE ACT

Strikers, they say, hunt in pairs. In the case of John Thomas and Gary Brazil the claim certainly applied. Between them they netted over 100 goals for Preston North End.

But this was not the classic combination of big fellow and side-kick, both were reasonably small in stature and similar in style.

Thomas and Brazil were, however giants in the penalty area and together proved a formidable duo, especially during the campaign which saw Preston North End finish runners-up in the old Fourth Division in 1987.

Midlander Thomas, later to have a second spell with the club in the evening of his career, was a folk hero - few players have heard their name chanted with more affection from the Deepdale terraces.

Southener Brazil, only marginally less popular, was a terrific servant over many seasons prior to a big money transfer to Newcastle. It could be argued that both had their best spells while wearing North End colours.

In that aforementioned elevation season which also saw league crowds reach 16,000 plus, Thomas and Brazil bagged close on 50 goals; Thomas had recorded a hat-trick of hat-tricks before Christmas.

Thomas, the undisputed King of the Kop, cost just £15,000 when he arrived from Lincoln in the summer of '85. He left to join Bolton before returning for a £50,000 fee from West Brom in 1990.

Brazil also joined in '85, initially on loan and then eventually as part of a £22,000 deal with Sheffield United which also included Bob Atkins.

If strikers are judged on goals scored then both can consider themselves highly succesful with North End - Thomas netted 44 in 105 league games while Brazil managed 58 in 166.

At the start of the 1992/93 season the two old P.N.E. colleagues were still alive and kicking - and scoring! – Brazil with Fulham and Thomas with Halifax.

Gary Brazil (left) and John Thomas two of the most popular PNE players in modern times.

119 mins 30 secs

April 30th 1938. Just 12 months after appearing in their first Wembley final Preston North End were back again with a point to prove.

2.58 Tom Smith wins the toss and Preston are off in attack right away. Delightful stuff being played along the ground.
3.05 Mutch breaks through but falls in the penalty area. No penalty given.
3.12 Tom Smith clears from Isaac but there are signs of strain in the North End defence.
3.21 Let-off for Preston. Holdcroft saves well from Barclay.
3.25 Bobby Beattie almost does it for P.N.E. but Hesford clears.
3.27 Now its humming. Shankly sends Watmough clear but his cross is wasted by O'Donnell.

3.43 Holdcroft makes a full length save from Beasley.
Half-Time: 0-0.
4.08 Preston swap things about, Maxwell and O'Donnell change places.
4.13 Mutch hits the crossbar.
4.25 Hesford makes a point blank save from Bobby Beattie.
4.30 Mutch takes a nasty crack on the shin and is limping.
Full-Time: 0-0.
4.52 Watmough is up-ended in the penalty area, nothing given.
5.02 Holdcroft tips a shot from Beasley over the bar.
5.10 Hesford makes an acrobatic save from Bill Shankly.
5.14 At last! Mutch is through. No! He is brought down in the area. Referee Jewell points to the spot. Mutch picks himself up and takes the kick himself. It's a goal in off the underside of the crossbar, with just thirty seconds of the game left.

That's how the cup was won.

George Mutch's winning goal with almost the last kick of the game.

This account is how a contempary journalist summarised the afternoon's dramatic events which led to the F.A. Cup coming to Preston for the first time this century.

North End line-up (versus Huddersfield Town): Holdcroft, Gallimore, Beattie(A), Shankly, Smith, Batey, Watmough, Mutch, Maxwell, Beattie(R) and O'Donnell.

CHARLIE

Charlie Wayman was a centre forward who just loved scoring goals. He had already scored over 100 league goals with his two previous clubs, Southampton and Newcastle prior to his signing as a 29 year old in 1950.

He proved if you were good enough you were big enough, he was only 5'5½" tall, by no means the ideal height for a centre forward according to most judges of soccer.

He scored his first North End goal in his third game in front of a 44,277 crowd at Notts. County. Clubs would be happy with half that gate nowadays.

During the Second Division Championship Season of 1950/51 Charlie scored all four North End goals in a 4-1 win against Queens Park Rangers at Loftus Road on Christmas Day.

Charlie benefited from the fact that a certain Tom Finney was the goal-maker-in-chief at the time, but chances still have to be put away.

His courage made him a real favourite at Deepdale often scoring against the odds when up against centre halves a good six inches taller than himself.

Charlie got himself into the record books when during the 1953/54 F.A. Cup run he scored in every round including the final against West Bromwich Albion.

Charlie's scoring record at North End is second to none, hitting the net a remarkable 117 times in only 171 league games. That averages 2 goals in every 3 games.

Charlie Wayman not the tallest centre forward but one of the most effective.

Charlie Wayman scoring in the 1954 F.A.Cup Final against West Bromwich Albion.

LITTLE DEMON

Jimmy Ross was a phenominal goalscorer whose strike rate makes modern day 'prolific' goalscorers records look quite ordinary. Jimmy, one of the "Old Invincibles", was unlucky in the fact that his four best seasons were in pre-league days otherwise he would easily hold all North End goalscoring records.

From 1884 to 1888 he had scored over 250 goals in only 220 games; a brilliant return whatever era he played in. He forged a successful partnership with Johnny Goodall, England's centre forward in the 1880's as North End were at the forefront of the soccer world.

Jimmy would have undoubtedly played for Scotland had the selectors not enforced the blinkered rule of only selecting players actually playing in Scotland.

He was a big match player delivering the goods in the games where it mattered. He had the distinction of scoring goals for Preston in both F.A.Cup and Lancashire Cup Finals.

Jimmy played and scored in North End's two biggest wins, 26-0 versus Hyde and 18-0 versus Reading. He apparently scored seven against Hyde and six against Reading. In thirty seven F.A. Cup ties he scored 39 goals, easily a Preston North End record.

Jimmy, the "Little Demon", as he was nicknamed, was exceptionally sharp around the goals and had deadly shooting power for such a slightly built man. After eleven years at Deepdale he went onto play for Liverpool, Manchester City and Burnley.

Jimmy Ross - scorer of 39 goals in 37 F.A. Cup games.

1964

No matter what anyone paid for a Wembley ticket, it was cheap at the price.

There have been many highs in the topsy-turvy life of Preston North End and their performance in reaching the 1964 F.A. Cup Final, as a Second Division club, was an achievement in itself.

To then participate in one of the classic finals was a further plus although, ultimately, the day ended in disappointment - dramatic, painful and cruel disappointment at that.

A stirring game of football mixing graceful movement, colourful enthusiasm and sustained excitement, this was a spectacle of the highest order.

As one commentator put it: "Officials would have been justified and applauded for awarding a cup to both teams."

That West Ham won in injury time was a crushing climax for the determined North End players who had twice held the lead. Much of the pre-match controversy had centred around P.N.E. and two of their players, regular left half Ian Davidson and seventeen year old Howard Kendall.

North End dropped an eve-of-Final bombshell by dropping Davidson and naming Kendall, then to become the youngest ever to appear in the event, in their starting line-up.

Manager Jimmy Milne explained that Davidson had missed a League game against Northhampton in order to attend the funeral of an uncle in Edinburgh. Apparently there had been no such funeral and North End took action by disciplining the player. The ultimate price was his Wembley place and Kendall, a cool teenager who had just captained England to success in a major International youth tournament in Holland, was handed a dream chance.

He turned in a wonderfully precocious performance and had a major part in North End taking the lead.

Holden strokes in Preston's first goal.

Dawson heads home Wilson's corner for North End's second.

Injured Kelly can only watch Boyce head West Ham's winner.

Howard Kendall, at 17 was the youngest player to appear in a Cup Final, pictured with 18 year old John Sissons.

Kendall's pass set up Alex Dawson whose shot spilled out of Jim Standen's hands only for Doug Holden to score from close range.

A minute later Johnny Sissons worked a superb interchange of passes jinked inside a defensive challenge and clipped a shot out of the reach of Alan Kelly.

Neither team gave any hint of any dark or defensive thoughts and the game continued free and open. The power of Dawson, a constant menace, brought Preston the lead again when he rose to head home a corner, but the drama was only just beginning.

Fortune favoured West Ham early in the second half when Geoff Hurst smashed in a shot which Kelly instinctively pushed onto the crossbar only to see the ball come down, hit him on the back and trickle over the line.

Encouraged, the Hammers swept ceaselessly on goal, looking to take control. But, in spite of much enforced defending, North End continued to look lively and likely on the break. Dawson and Holden both might have fared better from good positions until a late, late decider settled it in favour of the Londoners.

In the second minute of injury time Ronnie Boyce strode forward almost the first time on the afternoon and headed home the goal which silenced the Preston hordes.

Many Press scribes felt North End had been desperately unlucky in what was called at the time "The best Post-War Cup Final aside from Manchester United's marvellous victory over Blackpool in 1948."

It was Preston who got the credit for making it a match to savour.

As the Division Two underdogs they had surprised the majority through their unexpected aggressive resistance.

West Ham: Standen, Bond, Burkett, Bovington, Brown, Moore(capt.), Brabrook, Boyce, Byrne, Hurst, Sissons.
Preston North End: Kelly, Ross, Smith, Lawton(capt.), Singleton, Kendall, Wilson, Ashworth, Dawson, Spavin, Holden.
West Ham United (1) 3, Preston North End (2) 2.
Sissons, Hurst, Boyce. Holden, Dawson.
Attendance 100,000. Receipts £89,000.

JOE McCALL

Joe McCall cost P.N.E. £5 when he signed on from nearby Kirkham F.C. in 1906 and he loyally stayed at Deepdale until 1925. During that time he became a household name in the annals of soccer as a hard but fair top class defender playing 370 league games for the club.

He started his Preston career slowly only playing a handful of games in his first couple of seasons before making his mark as North End's centre half.

He was an aggressive, wholehearted attacking type of defender who was masterful in the air even though he was relatively small for his position, standing 5'8½" tall.

His playing career was in two halves, as the First World War disrupted life in general. During the 1912/13 season Joe was chosen to play for England and he scored on his debut in a 4-3 win against Wales - the same season North End were crowned 2nd Division Champions.

Joe was proudly appointed captain of Preston North End from the 29th November 1913 after his defensive partner, Eddie Holdsworth, had asked for a transfer. Up to the war breaking out Joe had played 211 league games for P.N.E.

After the war Joe, a born leader, led North End to the 1922 F.A. Cup Final but was unfortunately the losing captain.

Joe was good enough to appear for England both before and after the war and if the Footballer of the Year trophy had been around, then he would have no doubt been a recipient of the award, as he was as famous in his day as Tom Finney was in his.

Joe McCall - loyal servant of the club for almost 20 years.

Kept in the dark

On 26th September 1938 P.N.E. took part in the Charity Shield. For some reason the game was played at Highbury, the home of their opponents Arsenal, in almost total darkness.

The F.A. Cup holders and the League Champions were expected to produce a fine exhibition of football and it was hoped to attract a crowd large enough to provide £1,000 for charities. Unfortunately the attendance was only 7,233 with receipts being £545-10s.

It was reported that the "political crisis" was largely responsible for the match failing as a spectacle.

Long before the ball was set into motion it was so dark on the field that both goals were obscured. It was reported that people were burning newspapers on the terraces to use as torches.

Arsenal won the game 2-1 scoring twice in the first five minutes - both goals coming from Ted Drake.

North End's goal was apparently scored by Bobby Beattie in the 79th minute.

The game itself was taken lightly by the players which was understandably due to the farcical conditions they were forced to play in.

The F.A. officials at the match merely met the players as they trooped off the field and handed them their medals. They did not even present the shield to the winning team.

Ironically the Highbury officials switched on the floodlights after the game was finished!

North End's forward trio of Mutch, Dougal and R. Beattie (scorer of Preston's goal).

A GOOD HYDING

North End hold a record which is unlikely ever to be broken. They beat a Hyde United side in the F.A. Cup by a staggering 26-0.

Dewhurst
3

Graham
1

Goodall
1

Drummond
2

Thomson
5

Russell
1

J. Ross
7

Gordon
5

N. Ross
1

On the 15th October 1887 a game took place at Deepdale which was to be written into soccer history books and remain there for years to come. It was that 26-0 game most schoolboys hear about from their fathers and grandfathers. It was no exception. Did all the team score and who got the most goals? These were just two questions I wanted answering as a schoolboy.

Only a "fair muster" of spectators assembled at Deepdale for this English Cup First Round tie against the Hyde club from the Manchester area. Sam Thomson turned out for his first game of the season and took his place at the front. Fred Dewhurst got the ball rolling, scoring the game's first goal with less than five minutes gone.

It was twenty five minutes before Addison, North End's goalkeeper, got his first touch of the ball, by which time Drummond, J.Ross and Dewhurst had added to the scoreline.

Within five minutes another three goals were in the bag from the likes of Drummond, Graham and Thomson. North End's right wing then got into the act with Gordon and J.Ross grabbing goals eight and nine.

Double figures were reached when Nick Ross came up from full-back to blast one past Bunyan, Hyde's goalkeeper. Before the bemused crowd had stopped applauding Thomson and Gordon had made it 12-0. All before half time. Talk about one way traffic!

By this time the match reporter's pencil must have been blunt and all he could do to keep pace was to record the goalscorers as the total totted up to that now famous 26-0 scoreline.

A hundred years on, to commemorate the famous win, North End played an exhibition match at Hyde. Despite a replica kit and a few centre partings, the score was a more respectable 4-1 win.

For the budding statisticians the second half goalscorers were: Thomson, Thomson, J. Ross, Thomson, J.Ross, J.Ross, Gordon, Russell, J.Ross, Gordon, Gordon, Dewhurst, J.Ross and finally, Goodall.

Just for the record Bob Howarth, North End's right back, did not manage to score. And the goalkeeper, Addison, was said to have had a quiet game.

T.T.

England International Tommy Thompson proved to be a good buy when snapped up for £27,000 from Aston Villa in 1955. The free-scoring inside forward took less than 2 minutes to score on his Preston North End debut at Everton in a 4-0 win.

Tommy soon won the admiration of the Deepdale crowds, helped by the fact that he scored five times in his first six games for the club.

He immediately formed a successful right-wing partnership with Tom Finney and the two Tommies went on to score 203 First Division goals between them in just five seasons.

On a personal note, Tommy's season was 1957/58 when he created a new P.N.E. goal scoring record for the first division, in scoring 34 goals. If he had taken the team's penalties he would have probably set up North End's all-time record for most goals in the season.

When capped for England he had the honour of playing between Stan Matthews and Tom Finney against Scotland at Wembley. Tommy captained Preston North End when the club undertook a tour of South Africa in 1958, winning 7 out of the 9 games played.

His goal scoring record whilst at Deepdale was that he played in 209 League and Cup games scoring 126 goals, a very good return from a very good professional.

Tommy Thompson, holder of North End's First Division goal scoring record. He found the net 34 times in season 1957/58.

WEE ALEX

Alex James, one of the pre-war "superstars", was introduced to English League football when Preston North End bought him from Raith Rovers for £3,150 in 1925.

Alex James, another famous figure for Madame Tussaud's, and posing again with the squad (inset).

Over the next four seasons, this stocky inside forward with long baggy shorts was soon to bring the crowds flocking back to Deepdale to see his artistic dribbling skills and his brilliant ball control which was used to engineer many a vital goal for the club.

His North End debut is best forgotten as we lost 5-1 at Middlesbrough and through a clerical error the club was fined 10 guineas, for he was registered after the game was played.

Alex's genius was soon recognised by the Scottish International selectors, playing four times for his country whilst a North End player, including one game at Wembley where Scotland romped home by 5 goals to 1 with "Wee Alex" apparently masterminding the victory.

For a scheming midfielder he scored his fair share of goals for Preston North End, 53 in 147 appearances.

He was later transferred to Arsenal and the big city lights where he was instrumental in bringing success to the London club.

A Whole New Ball Game

After Relegation to the Third Division, Alan Ball took only twelve months to restore P.N.E. to their former standing.

Alan Ball (senior), a craggy determined and ruthless manager, was given the chance to brush away the cobwebs within weeks of North End's humiliating relegation to Division 3 in 1970 – twelve months months later Ball had worked a miracle as P.N.E. were elevated back to former pastures at the first attempt.

Promotion was sealed against Fulham at Craven Cottage - thanks to a goal from Ricky Heppolette - and the Championship clinched just three days later, before a remarkable

Richard Heppolette.

28,244 Deepdale audience who watched Rotherham crushed 3-0.

Here we look at both games:-

At Craven Cottage on May Day, North End faced a Fulham side topping the table, the Londoners needing only a draw from their final match to make the title. North End lying second with a game in hand, had other ideas.

BBC Match of the Day cameras only added to the drama and P.N.E. lined up:- Kelly, Ross, McNab, Bird, Hawkins, Spavin, Heppolette, Ham, Lloyd, Spark, Clark. Sub: Wilson.

P.N.E.'s early pressing had Fulham pinned back and the relentless attacking paid full dividend on 22 minutes when Heppolette ghosted in from an inside left position to meet a corner and score with a superb diving header.

Fulham were sparked into immediate response and the visitors were asked to defend for some time. Fulham's fight and skill brought some anxious moments, Alan Kelly had to be at his very best and goal hero Heppolette made a goal line clearance.

Ball ran onto the pitch at the whistle to embrace his players - but the celebrations were only just starting.

The visit of Rotherham, who had stayed on the fringe of the promotion race without threatening to really get involved, were lambs to the slaughter.

Preston was ready to party and just short of 30,000 were not to be disappointed. North End won 3-0 and it was appropriate the 'Player of the Year' Alan Spavin should help himself to a couple of goals.

It is worth noting that aside from the magnificent effort by P.N.E., season 1970/71 had been a total disaster for Lancashire town football; Burnley and Blackpool were relegated from Division One with Blackburn and Bolton suffering in similar fashion from Division Two.

Alan Ball, his determination helped North End bounce straight back to Division Two.

Little wonder that Ball had become something of a folk hero in Preston, and club Captain Spavin was reckoned to have enjoyed his best ever season; other notable contributions coming from Kelly, Graham Hawkins, Gerry Ingram and Bobby Ham.

Alan Spavin, the two goal hero of the championship clinching match, prefers to celebrate with a cuppa!

KENDALL

A midfield general who hailed from Tyneside, joined Preston North End in May 1963 and became the youngest player to take part in an F.A. Cup Final.

It was North End's 3-2 defeat at the hands of West Ham in 1964. He was just 17 years 345 days - a record since broken by Paul Allen (West Ham). Kendall's League debut for Preston North End came 11 days before his 17th birthday in a 2-2 draw with Newcastle back on his native Tyneside. His first League goal came in the first season but the other at the end of the country, at Southampton in a 5-4 win.

Widely regarded as one of England's best ever uncapped players, Kendall's career was Roy of the Rover's material. On leaving Deepdale for £80,000 he starred in that great Everton midfield alongside Alan Ball and Colin Harvey. For seven superb seasons Everton played some scintillating soccer before Kendall moved on first to Birmingham and then Stoke.

Glory seemed to follow him wherever he cared to go and in 1979 he was appointed Player-Manager of Blackburn Rovers taking them to within a whisker of the First Division.

He moved into full-time management back at Everton and enjoyed further success winning the League Championship in 1985 and 1987 before trying his luck abroad as Manager of Athletico Bilbao. He was eventually lured back to Goodison Park for a third spell after a short stay at Manchester City.

Kendall played in over 600 first team League games. He was both stylish and a tireless workhorse with a great attitude to the game and a determination to finish on top.

Howard Kendall in his position as Young Lions Captain after victory in the European Junior Cup Final for the second successive year.

GEMMILL

A tough and rugged Scot born in Paisley, Gemmill joined Preston North End from St. Mirren in 1967.

Many of the superlatives and adjectives attributed to Kendall could also be attached to descriptions of Gemmill. He figured in 93 games before moving on to his best spell at Derby County when the Rams, inspired by Gemmill on the pitch and Brian Clough off it, took the game by storm.

He figured in 261 league games and went on to give outstanding value for money with Nottingham Forest and Birmingham. He had a short stay at Wigan before seeing out his playing days at Derby. Capped 43 times by Scotland, the first little competitor also participated in around 600 games before being reunited with Clough on the Forest coaching staff.

One of Gemmill's best games for Preston came in October 1969 at home to Leicester. He scored both goals in 2-1 win and gave a fine display. The goalkeeper that day for the visitors was the one and only Peter Shilton and the first goal was a header, no less, when Archie out jumped the future England star.

But it was his second goal that will be long remembered. A forty yard sprint beat everyone to the ball and he delighted the crowd with a goal out of nothing.

THOMPSON

Wing wizard Thompson had twenty clubs to choose from when he selected North End, then in Division One, as the club to join from his native Carlisle.

He arrived just at the end of the fabulous Finney era and made a league debut as a centre forward against Arsenal at just seventeen.

Thompson's rapid progress and incredible pace soon alerted the attention of other clubs and he moved to Liverpool for £40,000.

In 18 magnificent seasons and more than 700 matches he won 16 England Caps, 2 Football League Championships, F.A. Cup winner and runner up medals, an appearance in a UEFA Final, membership of 2 World Cup squads and a game with the League Representative side.

After more than 300 games with the Anfield greats he helped Bolton Wanderers back into the top flight with some exhilarating displays between 1973 and 1977.

On retiring, mainly through a knee injury, he severed his connection with the game and built up a very successful business empire.

Peter Thompson, an exciting winger who won almost every medal in the game.

Peter Thompson, Howard Kendall and Archie Gemmill, three players from football's Hall of Fame and a trio of players who kicked off their tremendous careers at Deepdale.

They covered the 60's at Deepdale, Thompson (1960-62), Kendall (1962-66) and Gemmill (1967-70) totalling around 320 games in Preston North End colours and notching close on 50 goals. All went on to great fame and fortune, including the International scene, but all remember with affection their early playing days with North End. Thompson, Kendall and Gemmill - three superstars for the swinging 60's.

0 to 8 in ninety minutes!

Jimmy Baxter kept the North End pressure on by dictating the middle of the park.

On February 1st 1958 Birmingham City made the 100 mile trip to Deepdale. Little did they realise that they would spend the full afternoon facing one-way traffic.

Tommy Thompson (left) and Sammy Taylor, the two hat-trick heroes.

Although Birmingham had only won 3 times at Deepdale in 22 visits, no one expected this landslide. Preston were dangerous from the onset, looking eager and lively.

They got a quick reward for an enterprising start with centre-forward Tom Finney scoring his 16th goal of the season, after 5 minutes play, coolly heading past Gil Merrick, Birmingham's England International goalkeeper. The accent was strongly on attack and with 12 minutes gone Finney scored in brilliant style. He waltzed past one defender, drew and beat another in a 20 yard dribble before picking his spot, scoring with a rising left-foot drive. The pressure from Preston was severe but the visitors held out until the interval, going in just 2-0 down.

The second half, however, was one-way traffic in North End's favour. With only nine minutes gone Jimmy Baxter at his scheming best put Tommy Thompson through to score his 22nd goal of the season.

On the hour Sammy Taylor missed a good chance, shooting wide, but within a minute he had the crowd cheering when he scored his 10th goal of the campaign with a header. North End did not sit but pressed forward and were justly rewarded with 3 goals in 3 minutes.

Not suprisingly it was Finney who set the ball rolling, for he had had the visiting defenders baffled with his artistry all afternoon. He cut in and set up Taylor to shoot P.N.E. into a 5-0 lead. Very shortly it was 7-0 as Thompson bagged another two goals, and there was still 17 minutes of the game remaining. Taylor completed the rout in the 81st minute scoring his 3rd and North End's 8th goal.

P.N.E: Else, Cunningham, Walton, Docherty, Dunn, O'Farrell, Mayers, Thompson, Finney, Baxter, Taylor.

ALAN KELLY

(AND SONS)

Great goalkeepers have been regular members of P.N.E. teams down the years...James Trainer, Peter McBride, Harry Holdcroft, Fred Else - and you could go on. But there can be little doubt about the most famous, most loyal, most consistent and most popular - perhaps even the greatest of them all - Alan Kelly.

Holder of the record number of P.N.E. League appearances (447) and 47 Eire caps, Kelly was respected the soccer world over for his ability, modesty, strength of character, pluck and cheerfulness.

A master of his craft who served North End consistently well for 14 splendid seasons, Dublin born Kelly's career ended on a sad note when he suffered a serious arm and shoulder injury in Second Division action against Bristol City at Deepdale.

Kelly didn't break through onto the first team scene until he was turned 24, when he made his debut in the First Division campaign of 1960-61.

His first appearance was an F.A. Cup tie against Swansea away on January 28th 1961 when he made the rush trip to South Wales after Else had fallen ill overnight.

Four days later came his League bow in a crushing 5-1 defeat at Sheffield Wednesday.

Signed from Drumcondra in 1958 Kelly made his international bow in a World Cup qualifier against England at Wembley. Again he wasn't blessed with a winning start, Eire going down 5-1.

Alan Kelly, holds the record number of League appearances for P.N.E.

After his playing days were over Alan Kelly was soon involved in P.N.E. matters of administration.

He was a coach and assistant to Nobby Stiles and also had a spell as a Manager in his own right in the early 1980s.

It was no surprise that two of his sons benefited enough from dad's expert tuition to make the grade as professional goalkeepers. Gary and Alan (junior) broke through in 1984-85 and 1985-86 respectively.

Gary started with Newcastle before ending up at Bury while Alan continued the long Preston connection by coming through the Deepdale junior ranks.

The two brothers played on opposite sides many times in third division action, Dad invariably a proud spectator, before Alan made a big money move to the Premier League to join Sheffield United.

Alan Kelly Jnr.

LOCAL HEROES

Nothing gives a club more satisfaction than when a local boy 'makes good'. Down the years, P.N.E. can call upon many examples... has there ever been a more famous case in football than one Tom Finney? In the modern era the list has added several names; Nigel Jemson, Alan Kelly and Lee Ashcroft to feature just three.

Jemson, born in the August of 1969, was a prolific goalscorer at school level who joined the Deepdale staff as a junior and never stopped scoring!

There was nothing particularly sensational about his first appearance - aside from the fact that he was only 16. He came on as a substitute during a 4-0 defeat at Aldershot in front of just 1,850 spectators on the last day of the 1985-86 campaign. His first full game was a different story altogether - at Swansea in January 1987 he marked the occasion with a truly memorable goal in a 1-1 draw. In his next two League games, against Lincoln and Halifax, he netted two more - a star was born.

Some 30 games later his talent had tempted Brian Clough's Nottingham Forest into a big money transfer and before long he had scored a Cup-winning goal at Wembley and won an England Cap at Under 21 level. He later had a short loan spell back at Deepdale before another massive bid took him from Forest to Sheffield Wednesday.

Nigel Jemson

Kelly junior, pictured left, was born in August 1968, followed in the famous gloves of his record-breaking goalkeeper father and again came through the junior ranks.

His first team debut came earlier in Jemson's opening season, 1985-86, on March 8th in a 2-1 Deepdale defeat by Crewe.

Kelly stayed in the side for the rest of the season, but spent the next five or six years - including promotion to Division Three - fighting various injuries and sharing the green jersey responsibilities with the likes of David Brown and Simon Farnworth.

He won International honours with Eire at Youth, Under 21, Under 23 and 'B' level and after some 150 games with P.N.E., left to join the Premier League Sheffield United at the start of the 1992-93 campaign.

Lee Ashcroft

Ashcroft, was born in September 1972, yet another starlet from Preston schoolboy football. A winger with skill, speed and flair, he starred at all P.N.E. junior levels before winning a first team appearance as a sub during a 2-1 defeat at Wigan on November 3rd, 1990.

His 'debut' came on February 2nd 1991 in a Deepdale derby with Bolton. His opening League goal was scored against Tranmere on the final day of that season. From the start of the 1991-2 season the exciting young teenager, later to represent England at Under 21 level, had become a fixture in the P.N.E. line-up.

The goal that took 275 mins

After 2 goalless draws on a bitterly cold night at Old Trafford, Peter Thompson finally broke the deadlock to send Liverpool crashing out of the F.A. Cup.

David Wilson. An exciting North End winger who, like Thompson signed for Liverpool, but later returned to Deepdale.

Beating Liverpool at Old Trafford in a pulsating F.A. Cup tie in 1962 still ranks as one of North End's most famous and rousing victories. There was much irony too in the fact that the P.N.E. starlet whose goal settled the issue was one Peter Thompson, later to play a major role in the development of Liverpool as a top European force. The original draw for the fifth round had taken North End to Anfield where a powerful, organised and gritty defensive display had earned a goalless draw; Willie Cunningham had been at his most resilient best.

The first replay at Deepdale had produced another pulsating encounter, but no player managed to break the stalemate - the closest to a goal came when Alex Dawson's blockbuster was cleared from the line by Ronnie Moran.

So 37,000 supporters headed for home trying to contain their excitement over a "third" clash to be staged at Manchester United. An even bigger crowd, close on 44,000 gathering at Old Trafford, saw Cunningham again lead from the front with a sterling performance as North End came under the cosh early on.

It was a bitterly cold night with a blizzard blowing across from the Stretford End, but the P.N.E. hearts were warmed after 275 blankety blank minutes with the all-important goal.

An Alfie Biggs centre was headed away by big Ron Yeats, but Thompson was first to react to the loose ball and roared in to crash an unstoppable shot past Bert Slater.

It was a reward for a courageous effort from the youthful Thompson and the veteran Cunningham.

One of the observers, Everton manager Harry Catterick, himself later to manage P.N.E., commented: "The boy Thompson looks a great player, even at 19 - he could be a successor to Tom Finney." Praise indeed.

North End lined up: Kelly, Cunningham, Ross, Wylie, Singleton, Smith, Wilson, Biggs, Dawson, Spavin, Thompson.

Willie Cunningham

Jimmy Smith

Tony Singleton

Three members of the North End defence that frustrated Liverpool for 300 minutes.

FIRSTS AND LASTS

Pontins were P.N.E.'s first ever shirt sponsors; Charlie Parker the first official manager and Bobby Charlton the first player-manager.

North End were the first team to win the 'double'. In 1889 they achieved it without conceding a goal in the F.A. Cup and without losing a game in the League.

John Goodall was the first player to score hat-tricks in successive League games for P.N.E. against Wolves and Notts. County in 1888.

Tom Finney, North End's most capped player, made his debut for England against Northern Ireland in Belfast on September 28th 1946. There were 57,000 spectators at the game which England won 7-2. Finney was among the scorers.

The first P.N.E. penalty was scored by Jack Gordon against Blackburn in a 4-2 win in 1891.

Tom Finney's League debut for P.N.E. was against Leeds on the opening day of the 1946-47 season; his farewell appearance (pictured above) came against Luton, again at Deepdale, on the final day of 1959-60 season.

Bobby Langton once scored a goal for P.N.E., away at Manchester City, after just 7 seconds.

P.N.E. were one of the 12 founder members of the Football League.

Arthur Wharton (right), born in Trinidad, was the first black player in English professional football. He was North End's goalkeeper in the mid 1890s.

North End's last First Division game at Deepdale was against Manchester United in 1961. A 4-2 defeat made relegation a certainty. Bobby Charlton scored the last goal, ironically, he was to score his last League goal playing for P.N.E.

The first and only time North End have had to apply to the Football League for re-election was on the 23rd of May 1986 after they had finished 91st. In gaining re-election they polled 72½ votes.

North End's first League Cup-tie was against Football League newcomers Peterborough United in season 1960-61. P.N.E. won 4-1.

The first televised Cup Final was in 1937 North End versus Sunderland.

John Thomas.

North End's first Football League game on 'plastic' came against Swansea at Deepdale on August 30th 1986. P.N.E. won in front of 4,377 fans thanks to goals from John Thomas and Oshor Williams. A season earlier, also at Deepdale, North End had participated in their first game as a Fourth Division outfit against Peterborough.

Osher Williams in action.

A Vale of Tears

Preston North End have encountered the 'Play-offs' just once, a volatile heart-stopping two-legged confrontation with Port Vale in the spring of 1989.

A place in the old Division Two was at stake and for some considerable time in the first leg it looked like North End could be set to accept a helping hand from soccer's wilderness.

Ultimately it was to be a "Vale of Tears" with Vale winning through on a 4-2 aggregate.

But North End fans will remember their expectations reaching heights of ecstacy in the Deepdale meeting when after just 15 minutes Nigel Jemson forced Mark Grew into a marvellous save before rushing on to toe-poke home the rebound.

Deepdale erupted and with North End buzzing Grew kept Vale in the game with outstanding saves from Tony Ellis and Brian Mooney.

But extra goals didn't materialise although Mark Patterson had one cancelled out on the strength of a linesman's flag.

Vale rocked North End on 67 minutes with a goal of stunning quality, a five man move being finished off in style by Robbie Earle.

The crowd of 14,321 then watched a see-saw tussle develop, but it stayed 1-1 with everything up for grabs in the return.

North End lost the second leg 3-1 despite another gallant display. Patterson was marksman, but Vale just possessed too much firepower on the night. An unused Vale substitute was one Ronnie Jepson, later to figure in an £80,000 transfer to Deepdale.

North End fielded identical line-ups in both legs: Brown, Williams, Swann, Atkins, Wrightson, Hughes, Mooney, Joyce, Patterson, Ellis, and Jemson. Subs: Miller and Rathbone.

Mark Patterson, scorer in the second leg.

Crowd favourite Tony Ellis was frustrated by the outstanding form of Vale goalkeeper Mark Grew.

Manager John McGrath steered North End from re-election to promotion in his first season at Deepdale. He just failed to take them up another division when they reached the Play-offs two seasons later.

SPAV

Aside from the legendary Tom Finney, Willie Cunningham and Alan Kelly, few have served Preston North End better than Alan Spavin.

Like Finney and Kelly, a one-club man, Spavin figured in more than 400 League games, an inside forward/wing half to compare with the best.

Some considered him too slow, they were wrong. Spavin was an artful, intelligent footballer of outstanding quality.

More than that he was a team man, a player's player. Spavin always worked ceaselessly for the benefit of his colleagues, a midfield tactician of an even temper who thought long and carefully about his game and was critical of his own performance.

Born and educated in Lancaster he joined the P.N.E. playing staff as a small boy of 14, the start of a career to rank alongside the finest in modern Deepdale times

He was a member of the F.A. Youth Cup losing side which went down to Chelsea on the famous night and went on to enjoy a dozen or so years in the first team.

As a talented young stripling he was thrust into a struggling and subsequently relegated First Division side, but the hard going brought out the best in his career. Spavin's heart was in Preston and he was a credit to himself and the club.

Many good judges claim that because he played his P.N.E. career almost exclusively in the Second Division he was robbed of international recognition.

He played in the F.A. Cup Final of '64 and scored two goals when North End clinched the Third Division championship in front of close on 30,000 delighted fans against Rotherham in 1971.

On retiring from Deepdale in 1973, he tried his luck with some success over in the USA with Washington Diplomats before returning to figure in three more North End games in season 1977-78.

Loyal and conscientious, 'Spav' was a great North End servant who fully justifies a place in the club's Hall of Fame.

Beating Reading 18-0

Gale force winds and torrential rain lashed Preston on the night of Friday January 26th 1894.
The following afternoon a hurricane hit Reading football club.

P.N.E. Vs. READING (F.A.CUP).

In 90 minutes of ruthless attacking, the awesome professionals of P.N.E. cracked 18 goals against the naive southern amateurs in the first round proper of the F.A.Cup. The visitors had been told in advance that the Preston 'Invincibles' were on the decline, dogged by injury and illness.

Reading's players complained in advance about the mud-bath conditions but Leek Referee Mr Armitt allowed the tie to proceed.

Reading won the toss but then lost just about everything else.

Reading held out for 18 minutes before conceding the game's first goal. Moses Sansers broke away, beating four opponents before passing on to Becton, and from his cross Barton rushed up and netted the first goal. Four minutes later and the landslide started with Jimmy Ross scoring the second goal. Within the next ten minutes Jimmy Ross and Cowan had made it 4-0. As one can visualise, the game was almost continually in the Reading half of the pitch and by half-time it was 7-0 with the goals coming from Jimmy Ross (2) and Cowan.

Three minutes after the resumption Jimmy Ross had bagged his 5th goal. Barton put on the ninth goal and double figures were reached when Saunders beat the keeper from long range. The rain began to fall and Nick Ross retired from the pitch, but North End's ten men playing with the wind put on another eight. Becton (4) Cowan (2), Barton & Jimmy Ross the marksmen.

In a match report of the tie it is alleged that the weather became so bad during the afternoon that Trainer, the P.N.E. goalkeeper, pulled on a mackintosh. He had just recovered from flu and was frightened that a soaking could give him pneumonia.

Finney's Nightmare
(The 1954 Cup Final)

Much of Preston North End's post-war history can be directly and indirectly attributed to Tom Finney; a match in May 1954 was no different - or was it? Wembley was the venue, the F.A. Cup Final the occasion and West Bromwich Albion the opposition.

Finney was North End's skipper and the focus of the football world was centred on him.

It seemed the ultimate situation, the perfect stage, but one point, so often missed, had been overlooked... Finney was a human being.

That May Day Cup Final, which saw Preston lose 3-2, was a personal disaster, Finney had what he later described as "a stinker."

So poor was Finney's contribution that the Daily Mail reported:- "Preston should forget all about the match - and try again next year, with a new Captain. So far as Finney is concerned, this would be a pleasure." A harsh verdict, but Finney never dodged the criticism or the blame. It was, in a nutshell,his worst ever game.

In front of the 100,000 onlookers North End fielded:-

Thompson, Cunningham, Walton, Docherty, Marston, Forbes, Finney, Foster, Wayman, Baxter and Morrison.West Brom included the inspirational Ronnie Allen and his 20th minute goal rocked North End back on their heels, but in typical fighting fashion, only a minute passed before North End were level, Angus Morrison heading home a Tommy Docherty cross.

In the second half it got better, much better, as Charlie Wayman took full advantage of a dubious offside "decision" to race clear and score with ice cool aplomb.

Wayman's strike - he looked at least 3 yards offside - meant that he had completed the personal feat of a goal in every round.

Joy turned to misery as Docherty upended Nicholls in the box and Allen stroked home the penalty.

North End keeper George Thompson was left with more reason than most to remember the winning goal, he totally misjudged a cross-cum-shot from Griffin and the ball trickled over the line for perhaps the softest Wembley winner of all time.

While the P.N.E. disappointment was collective, no-one felt defeat more than Finney.

Many years later the great man commented in his biography: "I let everyone down with a performance I have always wanted to erase from my memory. It was a nightmare."

POST WAR MANAGERS

Scott Symon took P.N.E. to Wembley.

Jimmy Milne (left) also took P.N.E. to Wembley, pictured with one of his predecessors Will Scott.

Will Scott	49-53
Scott Symon	53-54
Frank Hill	54-56
Cliff Britton	56-61
Jimmy Milne	61-68
Bobby Seith	68-70
Alan Ball	70-73
Bobby Charlton	73-75
Harry Catterick	75-77
Nobby Stiles	77-81
Tommy Docherty	81
Gordon Lee	81-83
Alan Kelly	83-85
Tommy Booth	85-86
Brian Kidd	86
John McGrath	86-90
Les Chapman	90-92

Harry Catterick receiving his Bells Whisky Manager of the Month prize.

3 managers who enjoyed enormous success as players. Tommy Docherty, Alan Kelly and Nobby Stiles (inset).

Claret

In modern times P.N.E. followers have stomached several disappointments. But nothing comes close to the empty feeling left by the events of an April night in 1988.

Burnley were the visitors in the second leg of the northern final for the Freight Rover Trophy.

The first leg, played out in front of 15,680 fans at Turf Moor, had finished goalless.

The following week - with a final appearance at Wembley, the prize up for grabs - the occasion was even bigger.

A crowd of 17,592, the highest attendance at the famous old stadium for seven seasons, turned up and the atmosphere was frantic.

The game saw North End dominate but Burnley refuse to buckle under pressure. Gary Brazil found the net for North End but it wasn't enough and at 1-1 the tie went into extra time.

Preston were still running the show but a lapse in concentration allowed the Clarets to move ahead and in the closing minutes they broke again to make sure of a trip to the Twin Towers.

North End - players, management, supporters and officials - were stunned into total silence. Some broke down and cried.

This was the ultimate disappointment, the end of a fairytale. So confident were many fans after the first leg that travel to London and overnight stays had been booked in advance. The optimism and confidence were sadly misplaced.

Four days later, with the scars still fresh the team went down to Gillingham for a League fixture and got a thumping, 4-0.

The team on that fateful night read: Brown, Miller, Swann, Atkins, Wrightson, Jones, Mooney, Joyce, Hildersley, Brazil and Ellis.

Subs: Chapman and Williams.

Lee Chapman at 37 and nearing the end of a fine career, described it all as his worst footballing experience. There were many on the terraces and in the stands at Deepdale that night who echoed those sentiments.

Crowd favourite Brian Mooney, failing to connect with a cross typified a frustrating evening.

and Blue

Warren Joyce, the North End captain. His dream of leading the team out at Wembley evaporated that April night.

Gary Brazil, scorer of North End's goal.

THE DOC

Docherty succeeded Bill Shankly at North End, signing from Celtic for £4,000 in the November of '49.

A product of a tough Glasgow upbringing, he had worked through Celtic's junior ranks and had served the Highland Light Infantry for two years in Palestine.

His North End debut came as an emergency outside left at Leeds, but he soon settled to his familiar position at right-half.

Rated a top-class team man, strong in both attack and defence, Docherty was popular with colleagues and fans alike. Capped for the first time against Wales in 1952 he left Deepdale in 1958 to join Arsenal for £20,000 following an internal dispute.

Remarkably he had figured in 324 out of a possible 356 games missing only 21 through injury and seven through the call of his country.

He was to return - as Manager - in the early '80s, but was unable to turn the club's fortunes around and parted company after just a few months.

The Doc's illustrious career took him around the world as a manager, coach, commentator and soccer celebrity, as he became one of the great off-the-field entertainers.

JOE MARSTON

Marston came to Deepdale in February 1950 and went on to play 185 games he also became the first Australian-born player to be selected for the Football League Representative XI.

He was recommended to North End by Percy Sewell who had emigrated to Australia. Percy initially wrote to Blackpool manager Joe Smith but the Seasiders took no action and Preston's gain was soon obvious.

Joe had started his soccer life with Leichhardt FC in Sydney and had represented Australia. The tall lean Aussie first played for Preston at right back and did not impress; rumours soon circulated that he couldn't adapt to the English game.

The rumours were wrong. After some encouraging displays in the reserves - at centre half - Marston got his chance when Harry Mattison suffered a broken leg.

The rest is history with Marston forming a sound rock for the club in around 200 League and Cup matches. Broad shouldered and powerful in the air he was a dominating influence. After closing his English chapter he returned to Australia.

WILLIE FORBES

The left half, Forbes, came from Wolves for £18,000 in the December of '49, spending six seasons on the staff. Not blessed with Marston's impressive physique, he was nonetheless a tigerish player who revelled in the thick of the action.

Along with the quick-tackling Doc, Forbes never allowed an opposing player a second to settle into possession. Tough and competitive, he relished a battle and came into his own when the pitches became heavy in mid-winter.

Like the Doc he was a Glaswegian - and proud of it - but he didn't win Scottish recognition (Docherty collected 25 caps). A short stay at Carlisle brought his career to a close and he continued to live and work in the Preston area.

Many a top name striker cringed at the prospect of 90 minutes in the company of Docherty, Marston and Forbes. Quite simply the most famous half-back line in the club's history. They represented the backbone of the P.N.E. side during the glorious years of the early 1950's.

They pulled on the North End shirt for a collective total of more than 700 League games and provided a man-made 'wall' feared by forwards throughout the land. All possessed different individual skills and characteristics but Docherty, Marston and Forbes were united in one particular aspect, to a man they were ruthless and uncompromising.

The Agony and the Ecstacy

CUP OF WOE... AND JOY.

In the late 1880's, Preston North End dominated the latter stages of the F.A. Cup with successive appearances in the Great Final. Two clubs from the Midlands, West Brom and Wolves, provided the opposition and North End were to taste ecstacy and agony... agony first.

Albion were the only team in the country North End feared at that time and the old bogey rang true again at Kennington Oval where, despite a goal from Goodall, the Northern side lost 2-1.

Bayliss capitalised on bad P.N.E. defending to score the critical first goal on 17 minutes, but from then on Preston dictated the play and threatened to run riot. Albion's keeper, Roberts, had other ideas and somehow North End were denied until the 50th minute when Goodall equalised.

Albion only managed a handful of shots in the game but another one found the net to win the Cup in the 70th minute. Woodhall saw his volley strike a post and then trickle over the line to leave Preston North End devastated and demoralised.

North End had lined up: Mills, Roberts, Howarth, Ross (N.J.), Holmes, Russell, Graham, Gordon, Ross (J), Goodall, Dewhurst, Drummond.

What the papers said in the summer of 1889...

MANCHESTER COURIER 25 . 5 . 1889

The best team won, for they showed much superior combination to their opponents, especially in the forward department.

LIVERPOOL MERCURY 25 . 5 . 1889

At Last, the most perfect, the most consistent team in the history of the Association game in England have attained their just reward, and are cup holders.

THE BIRMINGHAM DAILY

By their victory at the Oval the great Preston North End team has clearly established its right to be styled the Champions of the Association game in England.

THE DAILY NEWS 25. 5. 1889

It is only right that the trophy should fall to the celebrated North End eleven who for several years have been distinctly the best side in the Kingdom.

SEASON 1888-89

P.N.E. WIN DOUBLE!

NO GOALS CONCEDED IN F.A.CUP !

NO MATCHES LOST IN LEAGUE!

A FEAT THAT IS UNLIKELY EVER TO BE REPEATED

THE 1889 F.A. CUP FINAL.

Played at the Kennington Oval, London, this was to be North End's first F.A. Cup Final win. They had previously met and beaten their opponents, Wolves, nine times scoring 36 goals in the process, so one would have thought that the team was pretty confident before the start of the game. Hunter, the Wolverhampton right-winger came very close to scoring the game's first goal but luckily for P.N.E. the post was in the way. As it was, it was Preston who scored first, Fred Dewhurst latching onto to a rebound off the crossbar from Ross's thunderous shot. Eleven minutes later the game was literally over for the Midlanders as Baynton, the Wolves' goalkeeper, found a Jimmy Ross shot too hot to handle. Only 25 minutes of the game had been played. The teams only had a 5 minute half-time break before re-starting. Jimmy Ross, who had had a hand in both goals, was 'on song' and later in the game he made a good run and centre enabling Sam Thompson to knock in North End's third goal. When the final whistle sounded Preston North End had achieved the first ever League and F.A. Cup double.

Jimmy Ross (above), must have been North End's 'Man of the Match', engineering all three goals at Kennington, scoring the second and ensuring North End's place in history as winners of the first ever 'double'.

ODDS AND ENDS

Joe Dunn, P.N.E. stalwart defender of the 1950s, can boast a unique soccer record. Joe and his four brothers all made the professional grade. He played more than 300 First Division games for P.N.E. and once went into a business partnership with colleague Tommy Docherty.

Preston North End have used Deepdale as their football home since being formed in 1881. A record in the Football League.

Goalkeeper J.F. Michell was the first (and probably the last) player to wear glasses in an F.A. Cup Final. He lined up for North End against Huddersfield Town in 1922.

In 1909 the Ord Cup Schoolboy Final drew an 18,000 crowd to Deepdale.

Preston North End were disqualified from the F.A. Cup for playing ineligible players. This led to legalised professionalism in 1885.

In the '50s North End had two formidable full-backs. It was an odd fact that Willie Cunningham, the right back, was a natural left footer and Joe Walton, left back, was a natural right footer.

Joe Walton

During the War there was a Grimsby-based fishing trawler named 'Preston North End'.

Tony Hancock cost £80,000 when he moved to Deepdale from Burnley in the late '80s. He broke his leg in a freak training accident and later left the club without once appearing in the first team!

In the late '30s North End fielded a team with 9 Scottish players.

When North End first started playing football they played in red and white halves.

G. Drummond (above) playing for P.N.E. in the 1890s once got sent off for fighting but was later invited back onto the field by the referee and duly obliged by scoring 4 goals in a 6-0 win vs. Notts County.

North End were pioneers of 'overseas tours'... in the summer of 1929 they set sail on the S.S. Olympic for a trip to the U.S.A. and Canada.

GOAL MACHINE

John Goodall was one of the most famous of the "Old Invincibles" but even he would admit to learning a great deal during his four year spell at Preston North End, where he played with gentlemen similarly gifted in the art of playing top class football.

Goodall had good vision, could read the game well and was always tactically aware of of what was going on around him.

London-born John first appeared for P.N.E. as a 'guest' in November 1884, scoring against Burnley in a 3-1 win. He was at the time a member of the Great Lever club. He had joined the Lancashire club from Kilmarnock where he had lived since moving to Scotland as a youngster.

Goodall joined the North End Club for the start of the 1885/6 season and he had a very successful first season scoring over 50 goals in only 56 appearances.

During one game played in Scotland during 1887 North End were 1-0 down against Dundee Strathmore but the team eventually turned in a brilliant attacking display and went on to win 16-2. Goal machine Goodall scored 9 of them.

John was a skillful player being Capped by Lancashire before earning national recognition. He was selected to play for England against Wales in February 1888. He played alongside his P.N.E. partner, Dewhurst and both players scored in a 5-1 victory. Goodall went on to score 12 goals in 14 games for England. John starred for Preston in the 1888 F.A. Cup Semi-Final scoring three times in a 5-0 win versus Crewe.

West Bromwich Albion beat us in the final and some books credit our goal to Goodall when in fact Dewhurst scored it.

His league debut came in North End's first ever League game versus Burnley. Although he failed to find the net he ended the season as North End's leading goal scorer, scoring 20 in 21 appearances.

Once again Preston reached the Cup Final but Goodall failed to score in the 3-0 victory.

Besides "friendly" games the Cup Final was his farewell appearance in North End colours as he moved on to join his brother at Derby County were they stopped for ten years.

John Goodall. Scorer of over 50 goals in his first season at Preston.

The 1937 F.A. Cup Final, 1st May
P.N.E. vs. Sunderland

North End wingers Jimmy Dougal (right) and Hughie O'Donnell look to the Old Invincibles for inspiration.

This was North End's first Wembley final and they went into the game very optimistic of lifting the famous trophy. Preston's team was unchanged from the side that easily defeated (4-1) their usual 'Bogey' team, W.B.A., in the semi-final.
Pre-match quotes from the North End players included:-

Burns - "I travelled as reserve when Newcastle won The Cup, and now hope to be on the winning side myself."

Gallimore - "Our defence should be good enough to hold Sunderland's attack, as we did earlier in the season."

Beattie - "I am an extremely fortunate young man to have been chosen for Scotland and to figure at Wembley... It will not be for want of trying if we fail."

Shankly - "North End on their day are as good a team as you can find in England, and will give Sunderland a battle."

Tremelling - "The way we are playing we should just about win it. I don't think there will be any stage fright at Wembley."

Milne - "If we play in anything like the form we showed against Albion we should win... but Sunderland are bonny fighters."

Dougal - "Our attack is better than people think,..we should win."

Beresford - "If we hold them in the first quarter of an hour the game should be ours."

F.O'Donnell - "We have improved as we have progressed and they say we are now at our best. That gives us encouragement."

Fagan - "I am lucky to get the chance to win a Cup Medal in my first season in England and will try my hardest."

H.O'Donnell - "We are playing better together as a team, and will be full of determination to win."

North End took a 39th minute lead through Frank O'Donnell but a brilliant second half rally enabled Sunderland to turn the game their way, scoring three goals in the process. North End, this time, were thus defeated 3-1 in front of 93,495 spectators but promised to be back, soon!

MICK BAXTER

Mick Baxter. As P.N.E. Community Development Officer, he set a standard for clubs throughout the country. His death was a great loss to both club and town.

Baxter, who hailed from Birmingham, joined the P.N.E. staff shortly after his brother Stuart, also a central defender, had made the Deepdale first team.

Mick signed professional forms on his 18th birthday and within a few months he had made his full League debut at Grimsby on 5th April, 1975.

Early the following season (75/76) Mick took over the centre-half spot from brother Stuart under Harry Catterick's management and it was not long before he registered his first League goal "V" Hereford in a 4-3 defeat.

At the start of the 1977-78 season Mick found himself partnering Graham Cross, a very experienced player. Cross was a short term signing, but he helped Mick considerably and consequently the partnership helped gain promotion for Preston North End.

Another experienced player who helped Mick's career along was John Blackley the ex-Scottish International defender. Mick progressed into a powerful centre-back who liked to join the attack whenever possible and he was rewarded with 17 League goals for the club.

In 1980 rumours had begun that Mick was being watched and the question of how long we could keep hold of him was being asked. He was to stay for another season and clocked up his 200th League game versus Sheffield Wednesday at Deepdale on 14th April, 1981.

Although Mick started the 1981/82 season with North End he was transferred to Middlesbrough on 18th August, 1981 after playing just one pre-season Anglo-Scottish cup game. North End profited by receiving a clear £350,000.

From Middlesbrough Mick went on to Portsmouth signed by Alan Ball Junior but unfortunately never played for them due to his illness and had to finish his career prematurely. He died in 1989.

LAWRENSON

Lawrenson became the most famous of the three as far as International recognition was concerned, Capped 38 times by the Republic of Ireland, he treaded some of the world's finest football venues with a great Liverpool side.

Born in Preston and the son of Tom Lawrenson, a former Football League player who made one appearance for Preston in 1954 and also turned out for Southport, Mark figured in 73 League outings for North End between 1974 and 1976 before a couple of big money moves took him to Brighton and then to fame and fortune.

A young Mark Lawrenson who early in his career opted to represent the Republic of Ireland despite being born in Preston.

A cultured defender, a player who always seemed to have time in possession, Lawrenson was a member of a fabulous trophy winning Liverpool outfit who dominated the English game.

Medals and awards came his way season by season before injury ended his career prematurely. He later had a crack at management with Oxford United and Peterborough.

ROBINSON

Robinson, a forceful, thrusting and all action striker, arrived at North End as an apprentice in 1976 after an upbringing in Leicester.

The goals flowed from the word go and after just 45 appearances the big guns were alerted to the immense promise of the fresh-faced frontrunner.

Manchester City stepped in with a hugh bid in June 1973 and the sum, £765.000, still stands as an incoming club record. Robinson stayed just a year at Maine Road before his career took him to Brighton, Liverpool, Queens Park Rangers and Osasuna in Spain. On retiring - more than 250 games and 75 goals later - he entered into business and also commentated on Continental Radio.

SEVENTIES STARLETS:
Mark Lawrenson, Mick Baxter and Michael Robinson were to the 70's what Peter Thompson, Howard Kendall and Archie Gemmill had been to the 1960's.
If the latter trio were the swingers then Lawrenson, Baxter and Robinson were the superstarlets. Three players who came through the Deepdale Academy to carve out illustrious careers which, in the sad case of Baxter, was to end so tragically.

Football League

After a 1-1 draw at Wembley against Arsenal, North End had to wait three weeks before travelling the short distance to Ewood Park, Blackburn for the replay on 31st May 1941.

In the 1941 Wembley final, Fairbrother, P.N.E.'s keeper, had saved a penalty from Leslie Compton and within minutes Andy McLaren had opened the scoring for Preston. Arsenal's equaliser came from Denis Compton. This game was North End's 3rd final at Wembley in five years, thus winning one, losing one and now drawing one.

By winning the replay by two goals to one North End made it abundantly clear, according to match reports and results, that they were the team of the season in England. Although North End's display was not as classy as the Wembley final they always looked as though they had something in hand, able to step up a gear when, and if, necessary.

Bobby Beattie had opened up the scoring and apparently the team sat back thinking the job was done. The incentive required to step up the tempo came from Frank Gallimore, North End's full-back, who unluckily deflected Bernard Joy's centre past Fairbrother for a late equaliser, with the referee ignoring his linesman flagging for a foul on Shankly.

Within half a minute yet another Cup Final had provided a sensation - a fine surprise Dougal-to-Beattie goal without the opposition touching the ball from the kick-off until it was in the back of the net. This was the sort of thing North End always seemed to have in hand.

Besides two goal Beattie, Bill Shankly and young Tom Finney were mentioned as being amongst the game's outstanding figures. Tom Smith was the proud captain to lift the trophy.

War Cup Final '41

Jimmy Dougal combined with Beattie for North End's winner.

Frank Gallimore. After putting through his own net he must have been relieved to see North End go back in front in less than a minute.

Bobby Beattie scorer of both North End's goals.

CAPTAIN SMITH

Tom Smith only played in 50 League & Cup games for Preston North End, but in that short career he was Capped for Scotland and had the honour of being Captain of the club when they won the F.A. Cup, back in 1938.

Tom was signed from Kilmarnock in December 1936 for £2,850 as an eventual replacement for Bill Tremelling, North End's centre half and Captain.

Tom had tasted success in Scotland, playing in the 1932 Scottish Cup Final vs. Glasgow Rangers and also playing for the Scottish League vs. the Football League at Everton's ground. Tom had to mark Dixie Dean that day and prevented him from scoring, on his home ground too! Tom also won his first International Cap whilst with Kilmarnock.

He only played a handful of games in his first season at Deepdale but took over the centre-half berth for the 1937/38 season. As it happened P.N.E. finished 3rd in the League that season and won the F.A. Cup, beating Huddersfield Town with that George Mutch penalty. Three weeks before the Wembley final North End were well represented when Scotland played England in the annual International match as Tom Smith, Bill Shankly, Andy Beattie and George Mutch all played for Scotland.

After the 1937/38 season had finished North End went on tour playing in France, Romania and Czechoslovakia.

The squad cradling Captain Smith, cradling the Winners Cup.

Unluckily, Tom broke his shinbone in one of the games and as a result managed just one more league game for the club as the war interrupted life in the U.K. He joined the Police Force but still managed 106 war-time games for North End including the 1941 war-time Cup Final win against Arsenal. In September 1945 he returned to Kilmarnock as Secretary/Manager. In later life Tom came back to settle in Preston.

Tom Smith.
One of the many North End Scottish players to represent their country.

The Scout: 30—1 TREBLE

DAILY EXPRESS

THE VOICE OF BRITAIN

No. 24,208 — Tuesday May 2 1978 — 8p

NOBBY DAZZLER!

A great day as manager Stiles leads Proud Preston to promotion

By Bill Elliott

SOCCER great Nobby Stiles led Preston North End back into the Second Division the hard way yesterday.

The former Manchester United and England player did it while sitting in the stands at Wrexham.

For the Welsh club's 0—0 draw against Peterborough means that the East Anglia team stay in Division Three while Nobby and Preston move up because of a superior goal difference.

So 251 days after taking over as Deepdale manager, Stiles has proved himself a success.

His achievement sets him alongside Jackie Charlton as the only successful manager to emerge from Sir Alf Ramsey's World Cup class of 1966.

DRAINED

But last night Nobby tried to shrug off the personal triumph by turning the spotlight on to his players.

He said: "I feel drained. This must be the toughest way to win promotion, but I'm delighted for the lads.

"They've worked tremendously hard this season. They've surprised a lot of people with their play and their attitude.

End of the agony: See Back Page

"I'm sorry for Peterborough of course but this game is about losing as well as winning. I believe we deserved what we have got."

Nobby should feel particularly proud today because he has found success his way.

His old Manchester United team mate, Bobby Charlton, brought him to Preston almost four years ago.

When Charlton left the club after a row, Nobby stayed but rejected the manager's job. His loyalty to Charlton surprised no one.

Looking back on his latest success, Nobby weighed it against prizes like World Cup and European Cup medals and said: "I didn't think anything could mean as much as those achievements, but this does. I am experiencing a whole new set of emotions."

Nobby Stiles celebrating at home with his greatest fans, sons John, 14, Peter, 12, and Robert, 9

Storm over China warning

Russia the enemy says defence chief

By John Warden

A MAY DAY storm blew up last night over Britain's defence chief calling Russia the "enemy at our door."

Labour M.P.s are demanding the resignation of Sir Neil Cameron, Chief of the Defence Staff.

His remarks during a visit to China are embarrassing for the Government and add to the tension following Mr. Callaghan's allegation of "mischief-making" in the Defence Ministry.

This has strained relations between the politicians and the military chiefs.

While inspecting the crack tank division which guards Peking, Sir Neil told its officers:

"Some of our problems are different, but one thing is absolutely clear to us, and that is the growing strength of the Soviet tank force . . . We must share, I believe, our common experience so that we are in the best position to take on the Soviet tank force if this should ever be necessary.

"Our two countries are coming more and more together. This must be good, because we both have an enemy at our door whose capital city is Moscow."

Sir Neil, who is Marshall of the Royal Air Force and the first Chief of Defence Staff to visit China, was loudly applauded by the tank commanders.

But his remarks infuriated Labour M.P.s who demanded that he be thrown out unless he resigns at once.

Mr. John Ryman, Labour M.P. for Blyth, will call for his instant dismissal in the Commons today, while the party's vice chairman Mr. Frank Allaun accused Sir Neil of increasing the danger of nuclear war.

Senior Labour M.P. Mr Norman Atkinson, who is party treasurer, is to demand explanations for Sir Neil's remarks from the Foreign Secretary Dr. David Owen and Defence Secretary Mr. Fred Mulley. The incident is likely to be raised with the Prime Minister this afternoon.

Said Mr. Atkinson: "The remarks could put the skids under any prospect of an arms limitation agreement between the Soviet Union and the United States. I think

Page 2, Column 1

Sir Neil . . . M.P.s want him sacked

What about the day Preston North End clinched promotion - without playing!

That remarkable event occurred on May Day 1978 when P.N.E. returned from the wilderness of Division Three... thanks to champions Wrexham.

Wrexham's final day opponents Peterborough could only manage a goalless draw allowing third-placed P.N.E. to go up on goal difference.

The dramatic final day in Wales had almost been too much for most hardy North End fans - not to mention manager Nobby Stiles.

Wrexham goalkeeper Dai Davies had an outstanding game and at half-time Stiles, trying desperately to hold still a rattling teacup and saucer, said: "I don't need a spoon to stir this tea, do I?"

Hold the front page!

Afterwards, a relieved Stiles admitted: "I thought I had experienced everything in the game, but that was something else. I've sat in a dressing room before a World Cup final, I've lost a European Cup semi-final and an F.A. Cup semi-final inside three days - but that was the hardest 90 minutes of my life."

The Twilight Zone

Some of the game's biggest names and characters have donned the famous white shirt of P.N.E... Finney, Shankly and Docherty to name but three.

1. Roy Tunks

2. David Sadler

3. Francis Burns

7. Sammy McIlroy

8. Frank Worthington

9. David Johnson

In modern times, the last couple of decades have brought what might politely be called 'The Twilighters'; players who have arrived at the tail end of fine careers to enjoy success and suffer failure.
Ex-Internationals, in their number you could pick a team of Twilighters - how about this for a line up:

4. Nobby Stiles

5. Tommy Booth

6. Alan Gowling

10. Bobby Charlton

11. Neil Young

Sub: Temple

Sub: Holden

HANDSOME HARRY

George Henry Holdcroft, nicknamed Handsome Harry by the press, was born in the Potteries and kept goal for Port Vale when just 17 years old.

He had previously played for Norton Druids, his local junior side. Given a free transfer by Port Vale, he was quickly snapped up by Darlington where he stayed for three seasons before being transferred to Everton. The Deepdale management produced a brilliant stroke in December 1932 by signing both Harry and Harry Lowe (full-back) for a bargain price, from the Goodison club. Holdcroft proved to be a very consistent goalkeeper as shown by his playing in 172 consecutive league and cup games, starting with his debut at Southampton Christmas Eve 1932.

In his first full season he helped North End win promotion to Division One with many refreshing displays between the sticks.

Harry's skill, composure, agility and masterly handling, especially in the air, earned him the right to be named alongside the best keepers the club had ever had, James Trainer, Welsh International, and Peter McBride, Scottish International.

Ironically, the first time that Harry was missing from the North End line-up was due to the fact that he was playing for England against Wales on the 17th September 1936. He also played against Ireland the following month.

That same season P.N.E. reached the semi-final of the F.A. Cup but the week before the game Harry broke a finger playing Middlesbrough and so missed the semi-final and also the final itself against Sunderland.

The following season P.N.E. returned to Wembley and defeated Huddersfield Town 1-0 in the final - in goal was Harry, keeping yet another clean sheet.

After 263 league games and 26 F.A. Cup games he found his life interrupted by the war just as he was in his prime. Although he played occasionally during the war his North End career was at an end.

He eventually signed for Barnsley then played locally with Morecambe, Chorley and Leyland Motors. Harry died in April 1983.

THE BIG THREE

Jimmy Milne would qualify for special place in any Hall of Fame, in view of 50 year's service with P.N.E.

Milne, whose son Gordon also hit the soccer high spots, created a real 'first' through his Wembley record with P.N.E.

Jimmy became a fixture in the North End team, unless injured, and he established himself as a consistent player. With maximum effort he gave his all to the club, loyalty, pride and devotion being his main attributes along with his composed temperament and his strength in the tackle. He represented the club in 3 different capacities in Cup Finals - as a player (1937) as a trainer (1954) and as a manager! (1964). He later served the club as general manager and scout.

Jimmy Milne.
Player, trainer and manager in F.A. Cup Finals. A Golden service to North End!

P.N.E. Statistics: Played 233 League games scoring 9 goals. Played 22 F.A.Cup games scoring 2 goals.

That Derby Game

They still call it Deepdale's Match of the Century. Against a strong Derby County side P.N.E. came from behind three times to win by three clear goals.

Tom Finney said in his biography "I can honestly state that of the many marvellous matches I took part in that was the best. For sheer incident and excitement I doubt whether it could ever be bettered".

The match in question came on Dec 6th during the 1947-48 season with Derby County providing the opposition in a top-of-table Division One contest.

Both teams shared third place in the table with the Rams unbeaten in 10 games.

Finney was the P.N.E. ace, Derby had the genius of Raich Carter.

North End had hardly settled down before Derby were two up. Howe rifling home a penalty and Morrison cutting in to add the second.

A humiliating defeat looked a likely prospect until Preston decided to begin a steady fightback.

Harry Anders, normally Finney's understudy, but on this occasion his left-winged colleague, began to weave his own brand of wing magic and before long North End had pulled themselves round on to level terms. Anders was up-ended in the box and after the referee and linesman had deliberated for some time, Shankly scored with a spot kick. The game developed into a humdinger and under the stress of fast driving raids, mistakes were inevitable.

Both sides remained totally set on attack and the 34,000 crowd roared a united appreciation as the thrills came at one per minute, first in one penalty area and then in the other. Preston's pluck was rewarded with the equaliser when McLaren timed a run to perfection to score with a copybook header from a Finney corner. Derby regained the lead after 32 minutes when Morrison beat two defenders drawing Gooch off his line and then shooting into an empty

Angus Morrison pictured in the North End line-up, but on this day scored a hat-trick against P.N.E. Impressed by this display, he was promptly signed up.

Jimmy Gooch. Despite his team scoring 7 goals, he was kept busy throughout the afternoon.

net. North End's determination could not be extinguished though, and they levelled at 3-3 before half-time thanks to Shankly's persistence.

On the hour, Derby pushed their noses ahead yet again, when Morrison capitalised on a rare error of defensive judgement from Shankly to complete his hat-trick before the home side produced another equaliser from the boot of Beattie after quite brilliant work from the tireless Finney. Eight goals scored...and Preston not once in front!

The atmosphere was at fever pitch and non-stop pressure from the home ranks produced a grandstand finale. Derby just had to crack - and they did. Pandemonium broke loose when, 15 minutes from time, North End took the lead through McIntosh before the same player hit number six in a goalmouth scramble.

But, not for the first time, it was Finney who was to have the final say to write the last chapter on an epic game. With the final whistle imminent Finney took up possession on the half-way line before embarking on a zany run, leaving defender after defender floundering in his wake, to supply the simplest of opportunities for a gleeful McLaren.

Final score P.N.E. 7, Derby 4.
A game in a million.

100 YEAR LEAGUE TABLE

Despite their recent barren patch North End still rank highly in a table that was compiled to commemorate the Centenary of the Football League(1988).

		LEAGUE		F.A. CUP			
		Championship	***RunnersUp***	***Wins***	***Finalist***	***Doubles***	***Points***
1	Liverpool	17	8	3	4	1	53
=2	Aston Villa	7	8	7	2	1	39
=2	Everton	9	7	4	6	0	39
=2	Manchester United	7	9	6	4	0	39
5	Arsenal	7	3	4	6	1	32
6	Newcastle United	4	0	6	5	0	25
7	Tottenham Hotspur	2	4	7	1	1	24
=8	Sunderland	6	5	2	2	0	23
=8	Wolverhampton W.	3	5	4	4	0	23
10	**Preston N.E.**	**2**	**6**	**2**	**5**	**1**	**20**
=11	Manchester City	2	3	4	4	0	19
=11	West Bromwich A.	1	2	5	5	0	19
13	Blackburn Rovers	2	0	6	2	0	18
14	Sheffield Wed.	4	1	3	2	0	17
15	Huddersfield Town	3	3	1	4	0	15
16	Sheffield United	1	2	4	2	0	14
17	Leeds United	2	4	1	3	0	13
18	Derby County	2	3	1	3	0	12
19	Bolton Wanderers	0	0	4	3	0	11
20	Burnley	2	2	1	2	0	10

Source: 100-Nil. A Celebration of One Hundred Years of the Football League.

Table based on League 1888-1988. 2pts Winners. 1pt Runners Up.
F.A. Cup 1882-1988. 2pts Winners. 1pt Finalists.
Bonus point to teams that achieved League/F.A. Cup 'Double.'

A Grand Day Out!

(30th April 1904)

To have a Championship depending on a single result on the very last day of the season represents an exciting but nail-biting situation especially when your opponents are your biggest local rivals. There was such a game, if North End won, they would be Second Division Champions. Out of the previous seven League games, North End were unbeaten but had drawn 6 - this time a draw would not be good enough, a win was vital. The team chosen to represent P.N.E. included Thomas Rodway who was signed that week from Wellingbor-ough after having

Percy Smith (bottom row) scorer of the promotion winning goal. Tom Rodway (back row) made his debut in the Blackpool game, he went on to play 336 games for the club.

previously played for Aston Villa. He was a left back who went on to play 355 League games for the club, Percy Smith was brought back for the game after missing the previous outing at Lincoln.

John Bell won the toss for Preston and chose to defend the 'Barracks' goal. Although the early play was even, North End seemed over anxious, not showing their true form. Fine defensive play from Taylor and Rodway kept Blackpool at bay, but it was North End who broke the deadlock with a five man move, McLean and Bond got free on the right wing and fed Wilson who in turn found Bell. The Captain shouldered his man off and deftly placed the ball to leading scorer Smith, who scored with a superb shot from outside the area. North End, although not in top form, did enough for the remainder of the game to keep Blackpool away from Taylor's goal and gain the required win to land the Championship and regain First Division status.

Another Second Division title was to come North End's way in 1913 and again the Championship was hanging on a game against a local rival - this time Burnley. In a fabulous season - aside from one 5-1 roasting from Leeds - P.N.E. had bossed things from start to finish, at one point recording six successive away wins.

Promotion was there to be won at the start of April with opponents Burnley lying second in the table.

The fixture took place on a Thursday afternoon and according to reports, every cab and wagonette in Preston had been booked weeks in advance.

Mill workers were granted, or simply took the time off to be at Deepdale for what was a feverishly atmospheric occasion.

North End had to battle for a share of the spoils in 1-1 draw, Billy Luke scoring a fluke, and elevation to the higher grade was not mathematically certain until 48 hours later when P.N.E. won 1-0 at Leicester.

THE BEATTIE BOYS

(NO RELATION)

Andy and Bobby Beattie had plenty in common...both played for North End in the 1930's, both hailed from Scotland, both won International recognition and both were among the club's most popular players of their generation.

But, in spite of all those connections, Andy and Bobby were not related - a fact not necessarily realised by many P.N.E. followers.

Andy had a rags to riches rise to fame, being signed from Scottish non-League Inverurie Loco for the grand sum of £150, in March 1935. A month later he shone during a short Scottish tour and, as a result, made his League debut in the final game of that season at West Bromwich Albion, on the left wing.

Due to the competition within the club he then had to wait 16 months before getting another chance in the first team, chosen to replace the injured Shankly at right half, and had an 8 game run. The first time he was chosen at full back, at Chelsea in February 1937, he found himself in the right place at the right time catching the eye of the Scottish International Selectors. They chose Andy to play left back against the old foe, England, giving him the task of trying to subdue Stanley Matthews. He did just that, as Scotland won 3-1.

More was to come though, as P.N.E. reached the F.A. Cup Final only to lose to Sunderland. So in Andy's first full season he played just 18 League games but appeared in an F.A. Cup Final and had become a Scottish International.

He went on to win 6 more Caps before the war and he was never on the losing side. Andy was of a very composed temperament, a cool, polished full back who possessed good positional sense.

During the war Andy was in demand representing the British Army, Northern Command, Scotland Army and the F.A., as well as playing in 5 war time Internationals. He retired as a professional footballer in 1947 but continued in the game on the managerial front. After his Preston career he had spells with Barrow, Stockport, Huddersfield, Notts. County and Sheffield United.

Andy Beattie practising his left hook in the gymnasium! And pictured right in a more familiar pose.

He also had the honour of being the Manager of Scotland - twice! He passed away on the 22nd of September, 1983.

Bobby was snapped up from Kilmarnock in October 1937, for a reputed fee of £2,250. The day of his P.N.E. debut, on 9th October 1937, versus Stoke, he was just one of nine Scottish-born players in North End's line-up. The others were: A. Beattie, Shankly, Smith, Milne, Dougal, Mutch, F. O'Donnel and Maxwell.

Bobby was a brilliant ball-juggling inside forward with a football brain. Defence splitting passes came naturally as he set up many chances for his striking partners. Mind you, Bobby bagged his fair share of goals, scoring 57 League goals in 264 games stretching from 1937 to 1953.

At the end of his first season at Deepdale he found himself playing at Wembley in the F.A. Cup Final and came home with a coveted winners medal.

Another proud day happened on 9th November 1938, when he appeared for Scotland against Wales along with North End team mates Andy Beattie and Bill Shankly. The war once again took its toll, robbing Preston fans of what should have been the best seven years of his football life.

Bobby Beattie (second from left) lines up for a sprint in a training session at Deepdale.

Bobby hit the headlines more than once scoring important goals, none more so than the two which won the War Cup Final for Preston against Arsenal at Ewood Park. He also scored the goal in P.N.E.'s one and only Charity Shield appearance, also against Arsenal.

Once, in a game against Leicester City, two Leicester players apparently tried to sandwich Bobby but the quickwitted Scot stepped back abruptly, causing the two opponents to bang their heads together. Nice one Bobby.

Life was a short stay at Wigan Athletic before returning to his roots in Scotland.

North End's first ever League Game

North End's first League game was on 8th September 1888 at Deepdale, v. local rivals, Burnley.

The game attracted 6,000 fans anticipating a keenly fought match but North End were favourites to win going on past results between the two clubs.

North End, losing the toss, soon gained possession and quickly roared into a two-goal lead. Fred Dewhurst, after being set up by Goodall & Ross was credited with our first ever League goal after just two minutes play.

Many publications claim this was the League's first goal but in actual fact this game only kicked off at 3.50 due to the late arrival of the visitors. Jack Gordon had made it 2-0 within a minute of Dewhurst's goal. Although Burnley pulled one back before half-time they had no answer to Preston's inside forwards, Dewhurst & Jimmy Ross. Dewhurst had a header disallowed much to the crowds anger as the referee had awarded a free kick to Preston for an off-the-ball incident. Was there no advantage role in the early days?

In the second half, man-of-the-match Dewhurst crossed for the ever alert Ross to snatch the third goal, after which Burnley's counter attacks left more gaps at the back which were exploited and Ross scored again from yet another Dewhurst pass. Fred Dewhurst himself scored the fifth before Burnley clawed one knock in the final minute giving the game a 5-2 scoreline in North End's favour.

I wonder if the men who founded the Football League in 1888 had ever imagined that the competition would still be going strong today, 104 years on.

Fred Dewhurst, scorer of North End's first ever League goal.

MUTCH OF THE DAY

In his 1st season at P.N.E. George Mutch wrote himself into the history books in a most dramatic way.

Many professional footballers are remembered for a certain incident in their careers, Maradonna for his "handball" goal against England, Gordon Banks for his brilliant save from Pele and Nobby Stiles for his toothless victory gig around Wembley after the 1966 World Cup.

George Mutch also came into this category when he scored the most celebrated penalty in F.A. Cup history, the one that won the cup for Preston in 1938, in the last minute of extra time against Huddersfield.

Although born in Aberdeen he was signed from Manchester United in September 1937 for £5,000. George was a top class experienced inside forward who had the ability to shoot with either foot.

For a man only 5'6½" he scored many a headed goal, with a knack of being in the right place at the right time, the mark of a good striker.

In the 1938 F.A. Cup run he got his first hat-trick in only 11 minutes, including two headers against West Ham. He scored another header in the 4th Round, made the goal that beat Cup favourites Arsenal, at Highbury (5th Round), and scored in the Semi-Final.

Then he scored the winner at Wembley, placing himself firmly in the P.N.E hall of fame.

George Mutch showing the cup to the North End fans on route to the Town Hall.

Bluebirds Shot Down

On the final afternoon of the 1965-66 Division Two season, Cardiff City travelled north to Deepdale unaware that they were in for the hiding of their lives.
Nothing could have prepared the Bluebirds for what lay in store on what was one of the most memorable days in North End's history.

P.N.E. had experienced a poor season, only evading relegation thanks to other teams failing, but being free from all relegation anxiety and tension, Preston gave the kind of display that die-hard fans dream of but rarely see.

Ironically, Preston had only registered 28 goals at Deepdale all season. The first half was totally dominated by North End's midfield trio of Spavin, Kendall and Lawton. Spavin produced an outstanding display with everything positive being radiated from him.

Wave after wave of attacks brought about a 5-0 half time score with Ernie Hannigan scoring three of them, Nobby Lawton and Brian Greenhalgh were the other goalscorers.

P.N.E. maintained their supremacy during the second half as Cardiff failed to pull together the tattered ends of a defence torn to shreds. Over confident, Preston actually started to waste the kind of chances they had taken so well in the first half of the game. Twenty seven minutes of the second period had passed - goalless, when Frank Lee was upended in the penalty area. Brian Godfrey stepped up to score the penalty and started another goal rush which culminated in Godfrey scoring a rapid hat trick (72, 74 and 76 minutes).

Cardiff, completely demoralised, had been run off their feet, but more was to come. After several near misses Greenhalgh broke through to grab his second goal bringing the score up to 9-0, which is still P.N.E.'s record League score this century.

P.N.E. 9, Cardiff City 0.
7th May 1966.
Attendance 10,018.
P.N.E; Kelly, Ross, Smith, Lawton, Singleton, Kendall, Hannigan, Godfrey, Greenhalgh, Spavin, Lee.
Sub: Ashworth.

Ernie Hannigan

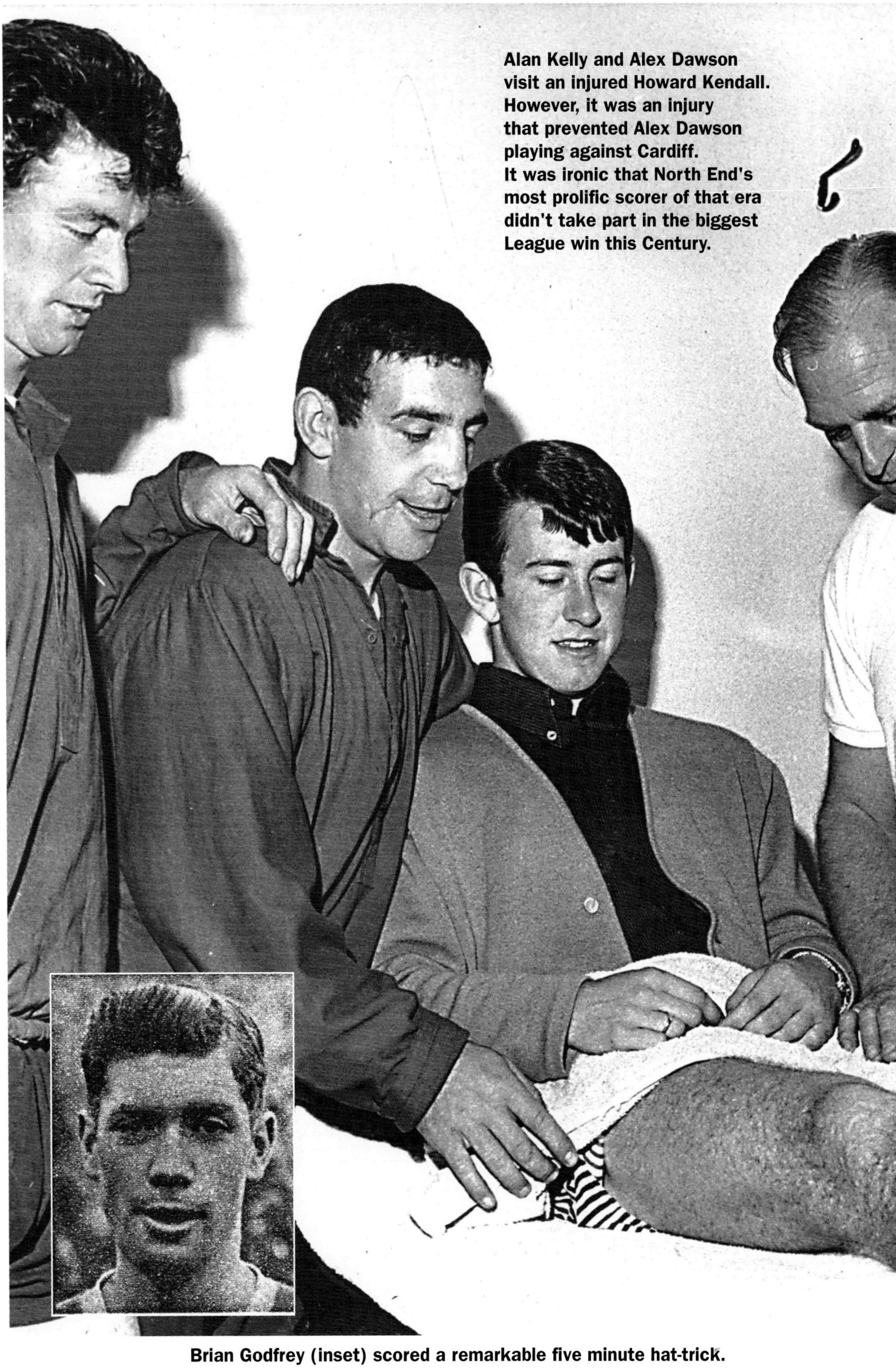

Alan Kelly and Alex Dawson visit an injured Howard Kendall. However, it was an injury that prevented Alex Dawson playing against Cardiff. It was ironic that North End's most prolific scorer of that era didn't take part in the biggest League win this Century.

Brian Godfrey (inset) scored a remarkable five minute hat-trick.

HARPER

Ted Harper was just what the doctor ordered, so to speak. North End were third from bottom of Division Two (Dec. 1931) and needed a tonic, quickly.

Dick Rowley and Ted were then signed in a double deal from Spurs as a last ditch attempt to salvage the season. Fortunately it worked, as Ted, a bustling centre-forward scored 24 league goals in just 23 appearances, lifting North End to a respectable mid-table position.

Ted, an England International, held the individual scoring records at both Tottenham and Blackburn Rovers at the time of his signing.

The following season 30 year old Ted carried on where he had left off, goal scoring wise, striking 19 times before Christmas including 4 vs. Burnley and 3 vs. West Ham.

Another hat-trick against Manchester United took his total to 25, then on 11th September 1933 vs. Lincoln, fittingly at Deepdale, Ted bagged 4 goals to break Tommy Roberts' record of 28 League goals.

By the end of the season Ted's total was 37, still a P.N.E. record to this day.

Just for good measure that season he, also scored 5 vs. Everton in a Lancashire Cup replay and another 4 in a 9-2 friendly win against Corinthians.

The goals started to dry up the following season and he was quietly transferred back to his first League Club, Blackburn Rovers, amid the minimum of fuss.

He had done his job well at Deepdale.

Ted Harper's tally of 37 is still a North End record for goals scored in one season.

WILLIE IRVINE

**The late '60s was not the most successful period in North End's history. However, Willie Irvine brought cheer to the crowd with some exciting displays.
His form won him full International recognition with the Northern Ireland team.**

Cheerful Willie was signed from Burnley in March 1968 for £45,000 in an effort to stave off relegation to the Third Division as P.N.E. were third from the bottom when he arrived. His Deepdale debut against Aston Villa brought him his first North End goal in a rare 2-1 win. It was only the third win in 20 League games, but in the very next game came another success, Huddersfield being the victims and Willie doing the damage with a hat-trick!

Whilst Willie was at Deepdale he was capped three times for Northern Ireland, scoring twice.

At the start of the 1968-69 season Willie set off in splendid fashion, scoring 16 goals in just 17 games.

Opportunist Willie happened to be finding the target but the North End team were still struggling. He received a knee injury during 1969-70 season and on recovering he was loaned out to Brighton and eventually signed for them in August, 1971.

Appearances-77+4. Goals-27(2 penalties). F.A. Cup: Appearances-3 Goals-2(1 penalty). League Cup: Appearances-7 Goals-4.

SMASH

Mike Elwiss was Bobby Charlton's first signing for P.N.E. He was a strong and aggressive forward with a ferocious shot.

Mike Elwiss spent four full seasons alongside Bruce... and what a partnership it was, realising in that short time 125 goals! Elwiss, a tenacious and willing frontrunner, arrived from Doncaster - marking his P.N.E. debut with a couple of first half goals at Carlisle.

On the final day of the 1973-74 campaign he got another brace in front of 16,000 plus at Deepdale, but it wasn't enough to prevent a Middlesbrough win and North End were relegated.

Strong and forceful, Elwiss was a great favourite with the fans but left in 1978 following a big cash bid from Crystal Palace.

His career at Selhurst Park never got the chance to get off the ground as the result of a serious knee injury. He had a short loan spell back at Deepdale but, tragically, in his mid 20s he was forced into premature retirement.

The full playing records of Bruce and Elwiss read:

Alex Bruce:
1971 to 1984, Preston, Newcastle, Preston and Wigan: 394 games and 167 goals.

Mike Elwiss: (League only)
1971-1979, Doncaster, Preston, Crystal Palace, Preston: 314 games and 100 goals.

Mike Elwiss. Forced to retire at the peak of his career.

N'GRAB

PROLIFIC... No other word could do justice to Alex Bruce's goalscoring contribution to the P.N.E. cause during the decade 1972-1982.

In 343 League games, Alex the Great hit the back of the net 157 times... a remarkable ratio of a goal every 2.18 games. And he didn't achieve that in an era when high - scoring matches dominated the scene, he did it in the face of disciplined and organised defences.

Born in Dundee, Alex joined North End as an apprentice in 1968 and three seasons later made his debut at Hull. The young striker served little notice of the future with a quiet bow - how that was to change.

The following season he was top scorer and he finished there again the next term, in spite of playing only half the games due to his transfer to Newcastle, one of many clubs to be instantly alerted to his promise.

After an unhappy stay he returned to Deepdale in 1975 in the deal which took John Bird the opposite route and caused Bobby Charlton to resign as P.N.E. player - manager.

The fans were delighted to have Brucie back. He immediately finished top scorer and repeated the feat a further five times before leaving for Wigan Athletic.

Bruce became a legend for his uncanny ability to poach goals from inside the opposition box. Only rarely did he strike from distance; his domain was close range and he was lethal. One observer once penned: "If the world was ending in a few minutes one imagines that Bruce would score before it did so."

Alex Bruce.
One of the most consistent goalscorers P.N.E. ever had.

The underdogs win their spurs

Undoubtedly one of North End's best displays in their long flirtation with the F.A. Cup came on the 5th of March 1966 - a magnificent 2-1 victory over mighty Tottenham Hotspur in round five.

North End, at this stage a Second Division outfit, totally belied their status to humble a team estimated to have cost eight times the total Preston valuation!

The following Saturday in the Official Programme (costing only 4d) the reflective 'Club Notes' read as follows:-

"Confounding almost all the prophets and upsetting Spurs manager Billy Nicholson in the process of wrecking his immediate ambitions, North End made last Saturday a great day in Deepdale history by knocking Tottenham Hotspur out of the Cup. The brilliant fifth round win followed success against Charlton and Bolton.

To add to the pleasure of the supporters, players and ourselves there was no question about justice being done by the result, which was fully merited on the play and the more to North End's credit because the Spurs, in an early break through, were given the lead by Jimmy Greaves. Our team took this shock in their stride.

The initiative was seized and firmly held, North End combined well as a team and displayed a most enthusiastic spirit which was maintained throughout an exciting game packed with incident. Alex Dawson headed a fine equaliser from George Ross's centre and Ernie Hannigan shot a second decider at short range following a partial save from Alan Spavin. We might easily have scored more. Spurs, despite the glamour of a team which cost a mint of money to assemble were well and truly beaten and out-played by a more determined and enterprising side which kept hard at it from start to finish. Tottenham were never allowed to take command.

In view of our present and somewhat alarming League position, due to the disquieting and rather surprising fact that we have not won a Second Division match for three months, all North Ender's sincerely hope that the matches ahead are approached in the same practical and earnest manner, and with the wholehearted endeavour shown in achieving the triumph against Spurs."

George Ross.
North End's long serving full-back crossed for Alex Dawson to head the equaliser.

1st Ever Match at Deepdale

North End's first ever game was always believed to have been played around 1880-88, but after hours of research the game in question was found to have took place a couple of years earlier, in 1878. The match report read:-

NORTH END vs. EAGLEY

This, the first match of the Season, was played on Saturday on the North End ground, Deepdale Road, and being played under the Association Rules, it was thought defeat for the North End was a foregone conclusion. A more even and hotly contested game, however, was never witnessed on this ground before. Up to half time nothing had been scored on either side. On the ball being started again, it was, by some very good play, driven up the North End goal, and eventually it struck the North End men, and rebounded through the goal, thus scoring the first and only point during the game. The play of both sides cannot be too highly praised, and it would be invidious to mention any particular player, as each and all played with remarkable energy and pluck to gain victory for his side.

Score:- Eagley 1, North end 0.

North End team:- W.Turner (Goalkeeper), Sudell, Sefton, Charnley, T. Wadeson, J. Wadeson, Miller, T. Parkinson, Dodgeson, Green and H. Cartmell (Captain).

This was an experimental game played by men who usually played cricket and rugby. No more soccer games were played until 1880-81 Season.

After taking part in the first game, William Sudell went on to become one of the leading figures in North End's formative years.

Tommy Thompson

HIGHS AND LOWS

For Arsenal's visit in a First Division fixture on April 23rd 1938, Deepdale housed its biggest ever crowd of 42,684.

In 1957-58 North End found the net 100 times, with Tommy Thompson (34) and Tom Finney (26) sharing 60. Fifty years earlier P.N.E. hit a 'ton' for the only other time in League action. Six players reached double figures.

Ted Harper's 37 goals scored in 1932/33 in 41 games, stands as the highest number recorded by a P.N.E. player in a League season. Only two other players have reached 30. Tommy Thompson with 34 in 1957-58 and Alex Dawson with 30 in 1963-64.

On the two occasions North End won the F.A. Cup they have only conceded one solitary goal (against Aston Villa in the 1938 semi-final at Bramall Lane, Sheffield).

The lowest number by a 'leading' scorer came in 1969-70 when Archie Gemmill topped the charts with 6. Jimmy Ross had the same number in 1890-91 but from half the number of games.

In reaching the F.A. Cup Final in 1887-88, North End scored 56 goals in seven rounds, but could only manage one in the final and lost to West Brom!

The highest attendance at Deepdale for a youth game was 27,764 in 1960 when North End played Chelsea in the second leg of the F.A. Youth Cup Final. Members of the team included (left to right) George Ross, Dave Wilson, Peter Thompson and Alan Spavin.

Alex Bruce holds the record for being top scorer in the most number of seasons - eight times in 10 seasons between 1972-73 and 1981-82.

Record receipts were taken at the F.A. Cup third round tie with Sheffield Wednesday in January 1992... a cool £68,650.

North End beat Stoke 10-0 in 1889 and lost 0-7 to Blackpool in 1947 and by the same score to Nottingham Forest in 1927... the best and worst League results. P.N.E. beat Hyde 26-0 to set an F.A. Cup record in 1887.

Alex Bruce

The lowest attendance ever recorded for a league game at Deepdale came on November 5th 1985 when just 2,007 watched a single-goal home defeat by Scunthorpe. The game was played on a Sunday afternoon due to floodlight difficulties. That same season the home League average gate was the lowest ever at 3,495.

North End's highest crowd during their two years in Division Four saw 16,436 pack into Deepdale for a promotion battle with Northampton on April 3rd 1986.

North End's record transfer came when Manchester City coughed up £765,000 for Michael Robinson in June 1979. The record purchase was Mike Flynn (above) from Norwich in December 1989 for £125,000.

The highest number of goals scored in one League match this century was 9 against Cardiff City in 1966. Ironically, it was in front of the lowest gate of the season, 10,018.

THERE'S ONLY ONE TOMMY ROBERTS

Tommy who? Tommy Roberts was the Alex Dawson of the 1920's. His goalscoring record is amongst the best of all North End strikers, scoring 179 League and Cup goals in 277 games.

Only Tom Finney can boast of scoring more goals for the club than Tommy Roberts, the Handsworth-born ex-programme seller.

Tommy signed for P.N.E. in June 1919 for a mere £400 from Leicester Fosse and what a bargain he turned out to be. In his first season at Deepdale he top-scored with 26 goals, the first time since 1904 such a total had been reached.

The following season his admirers saw him score no less than 8 hat-tricks, 2 of which were scored in the F.A.Cup as P.N.E. reached the semi's.

His goalscoring exploits led him to International honours, twice playing for England, scoring in both games. He scored a record 28 League goals during the 1922/23 season, followed by another 26 the year after - all in the First Division.

Tommy, one of the most popular and effective centre-forwards in P.N.E.'s history took only 167 games to score 100 league goals - a great strike rate from a first rate striker.

In October 1924 he hit the soccer headlines when he was transferred to Burnley for a record £4,600 fee, but within two years he was back at Deepdale, signed for a cut price £1,500 (Just how many players have left and returned?)

Tommy was soon back to where he was when he left - leading goalscorer - scoring 8 goals in his first 5 games on his return, and he ended up with yet another 26 goal total.

During May 1928 he made more money for P.N.E. being transferred to Tottenham for £1,000.

If the crowds chanted in those days they must have chanted: "There's only one Tommy Roberts".

NOBBY LAWTON

Many regard him as the best post-war captain. His inspirational qualities led North End to the F.A. Cup Final in 1964.

With North End struggling in Division Two having only 21 points from 26 games and with the transfer deadline nearing, Jimmy Milne (P.N.E. Manager) swooped down on Old Trafford and 'pinched' Nobby Lawton for £11,500 on 19th March, 1963.

What a signing he proved to be, quickly becoming Captain of the team, as he thrived on responsibility. He was a consistently strong driving force, always anxious to set the Preston attack into motion. He became a much improved player himself in such a short time and his inspiring leadership was soon to be seen by millions of television viewers as P.N.E. reached the 1964 Cup Final at Wembley.

Nobby was one of North End's bargain buys of the sixties and Alex Dawson his ex-team mate at Old Trafford once said of him "Nobby has the rare combination of class but bite." He was aggressive but fair, hard but not dirty.

He played 144 League games for Preston scoring 22 goals – 15 F.A. Cup appearances scoring 1 goal and 5 League Cup appearances.

Nobby Lawton. The last person to lead North End out at Wembley

The 1922 F.A.

Cup Final

In 1921 Preston North End reached the semi-final of the F.A. Cup only to lose 2-1 to Tottenham Hotspur of front of 44,668 at Hillsborough, Sheffield. The following season P.N.E. once again played Tottenham in the semi's, again playing at Hillsborough, but this time the score was reversed as North End won 2-1 to reach their third F.A. Cup Final. The last time being when they did the double back in 1889.

In the period between the semi-final and the final, Preston played 9 League games but did not manage to win one of them.

In fact the Saturday prior to the final P.N.E., by coincidence, had to play at Huddersfield in a League game and got trounced by 6 goals to nil. North End's line up for that game was Branston, Hamilton, Doolan, Crawford, Mercer, Williamson, Rawlings, Marquis, Roberts, Ferris & Quantrill. For the final itself, played at Stamford Bridge (Wembley was not yet open), North End made six changes to the team fielding Mitchell, Hamilton, Doolan, Duxbury, McCall, Williamson, Rawlings, Jefferis, Roberts, Woodhouse & Quinn. Most of Huddersfield's players had had the experience of playing in previous finals except Wadsworth, the left back, and W.H. Smith the left-winger, but those two were Internationals.

A crowd of 53,710 saw a rather dull final which the Yorkshiremen won by the solitary goal. That goal was a very controversial penalty given for a foul on Smith by Tommy Hamilton. It was controversial in the sense that the tackle had taken place a good yard outside the area and was clearly confirmed by press and newsreel pictures of the incident. And so the Cup was lost.

As most of us know, the two teams were destined to play each other again, 16 years later in the 1938 F.A. Cup Final where North End gained sweet revenge by winning 1-0, with a penalty!

P.N.E. vs. Huddersfield Town, 29th April 1922.

TRICKY DICKIE

Most soccer spectators love to see a tricky, confident winger in action, someone who can send a buzz of expectation around the ground.

Dickie Bond was such a winger. Preston born Dickie signed for his home town club during Preston Guild week of 1902, as a 5'5" 18 year old after some promising displays playing in army football.

He made his first team debut at Bishop Auckland on the 13th of December 1902 in an F.A. Cup tie and scored in a 3-1 win. His League debut came the following week at Deepdale against Stockport scoring again in a 6-1 win. The following season 1903-04 P.N.E. were the Second Division Champions with Dickie playing in a dozen games.

What happened to Dickie next was 'Roy of the Rovers' material. After establishing himself as the best winger at the club he rose to fame in leaps and bounds becoming the finest outside-right in the land in just over 2½ years. Trickie Dickie was fast and direct and caught the eye of International selectors, making his England debut against Ireland on the 25th February 1905.

He was the first North Ender to be Capped for ten years. 1905 was a good year for Dickie but he went one better in 1906 by becoming the clubs leading goalscorer with 17 goals as P.N.E. became First Division runners-up to Liverpool.

He went on to win 5 Caps whilst at Deepdale and another 3 after being transferred to Bradford City in 1909 for £950.

Dickie Bond. The dazzling skills of the Preston-born winger were soon recognised by the England selectors.

THE YOUNG PRETENDER

Peter McBride was brought to Deepdale from Ayr in December 1896 and was seen as a possible replacement for the ageing James Trainer, North End's 'Prince of Goalkeepers'.

Peter made his P.N.E. debut against Stoke towards the end of the 1897-98 season and went on to play consistently well for 15 seasons, before stepping down due to failing eyesight.

Peter was a classy, "keeper who represented Scotland six times in the days when only three Internationals a season were played".

The 14 stone Scot had a great reputation and a temper to suit. In his era barging the goalkeeper was common practice so his near six foot frame stood him in good stead.

McBride's loyalty to the club brought him next to nothing by the way of trophies, only winning a Second Division Championship medal in 1904.

At the turn of the century when Tottenham Hotspur were after his services he kept 15 clean sheets in 24 League games.

He went on to play a record 442 League games for Preston North End, a record which stood for a full 60 years before being broken by another great goalkeeper, Alan Kelly.

The famous 'St Peter at the Gate' photograph proved to be a popular postcard at the turn of the century.

Orient Express

Orient v P.N.E. April 1987: Les Chapman, who played on every Football League ground during a 700 game career described it as his finest hour.

Few of the 2,500 P.N.E. fans down at Brisbane Road that April afternoon in 1987 would disagree.

Chapman, then aged 38, struck the 82nd minute goal which not only earned a 2-1 victory but also clinched promotion to division three.

The midfield veteran, later to take over as P.N.E. manager, made an absolute nonsense of his advancing years to score his first goal in a year.

This is how the glory moment was described by the author in the Lancashire Evening Post:

"Chapman found himself in the clear heading towards the penalty area; he jinked one way, dummied inside a defender and dipped a delightful shot into the far bottom corner.

His scoring secret - FATIGUE! 'I was totally done in by the time the ball came through. Had the chance came early in the game I might well have snatched at it and the ball could have ended up in the crowd. As I was feeling leg weary I was able to steady myself - I was surprised to get so much power behind it!' "

North End had gone ahead inside five minites. Bob Atkins' long free kick had been flicked on by Sam Allardyce for Gary Brazil to bundle the ball home.

A foul by David Miller enabled John Cornwell's penalty to pull Orient level and the home side took heart from that 33rd minute leveller to turn the screw.

John Thomas had two "goals" disallowed as North End gained strength late on and Chapman's superb strike left the travelling hordes beside themselves in total ecstacy.

A pitch invasion greeted the final whistle and Chapman, manager John McGrath and the other P.N.E. hereos were chaired from the field.

Just two years earlier P.N.E. had tumbled into division four for the first time and then, a year later, had been forced to apply for re-election to the League.

Les Chapman. Scorer of the promotion-winning goal.

The achievement was granted a Civic Reception which turned into a non-stop carnival night on the streets around Preston town centre.

The P.N.E. line-up read: Kelly, Miller, Bennett, Atkins, Allardyce, Jones, Chapman, Swann, Thomas, Brazil, Williams. Sub: Worthington.

Sam Allardyce

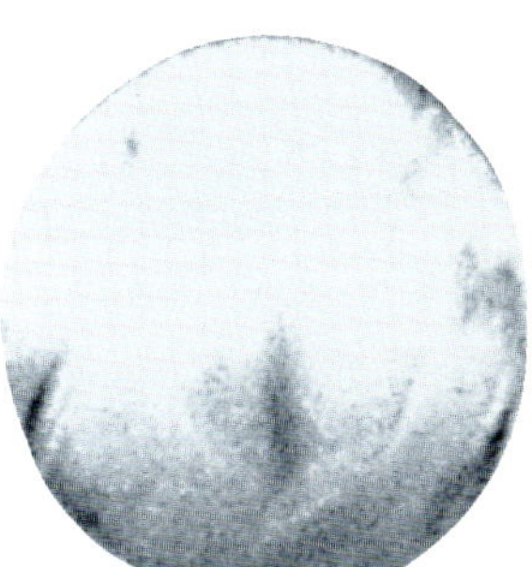

The two corner-stones of North End's defence, both had a hand in Gary Brazil's opening goal.

Bob Atkins

Celebrations begin shortly after the game in the visitor's changing room.

David & Goliath

So often have P.N.E. suffered at the hands of 'minnows' in the F.A. Cup... remember Telford, Whitley Bay?

But there have been occasions when North End have donned the costume of David and sent a Goliath tumbling in embarrassment.

One such F.A. Cup tie came on January 10th 1987 when 15,458 people turned out at Ayresome Park to see North End take the scalp of Middlesbrough in round three.

There had been much excitement in the previous rounds with North End opening up with a 5-1 victory over Bury before seeing off the challenge of non-League Chorley after a replay. The Chorley 'double', including a first game staged at Blackburn, drew in a total crowd of 31,461 - receipts of more than £80,000.

So, with 10 goals under their belts, North End went to Teesside with hopes high. The tie was in doubt right up to kick off due to treacherous icy conditions but it was 'Boro' who were to feel the chill come 4.45pm. The outcome was decided by a goal of stunning quality... midfielder Ronnie Hildersley's proudest moment in a P.N.E. shirt.

Hildersley picked up possession some 30 yards out, took the ball forward and ignored the temptation to cross by slamming home an unstoppable shot.

North End's huge following forgot all about the frost bite to do a conga of delight on the terraces.

Middlesbrough threw everyone into attack in the late stages, but this was destined to be Preston's day - a marvellous result for a line - up of: Brown, McNeil, Bennett, Atkins, Jones, Allardyce, Chapman, Swann, Thomas, Brazil and Hildersley. Subs: Williams and Miller.

Ronnie Hildersley

For the record, North End were given another opportunity to slay a north east giant in the fourth round, but failed to capitalise losing 2-0 to Newcastle United in front of 30,495 at St James's Park.

SIR TOM

What can you say about Tom Finney that has not already been said? He was probably the most complete footballer England ever produced.

A Finney

Matt Busby was once asked to analyse the relationship between Tom Finney and Preston North End.

His response provided the ultimate accolade: "The closest there has ever been to one man being bigger than a club."

Another Scot and ex-Manchester United manager - and arguably Finney's biggest fan - Tommy Docherty, described his former Deepdale colleague thus:

"The greatest footballer ever born. Di Stefano and Puskas were not fit to lace his boots - and he was way ahead of Stanley Matthews too."

Some tribute - but then more or less everyone, expert, player, commentator or supporter, seemed to see it that way.

Finney was a football superstar, a legend, a one off talent who served

old game

North End so well as a player in the golden years and stayed loyal in later life as an active President.

It would be impossible to do justice to Finney's career in a few short paragraphs. Suffice to say that he was possibly the finest English footballer ever.

Not only a spectacular player on the ball with dazzling skills on the wings, he was also an outstanding goalscorer, 30 for England and 210 for P.N.E. in 14 fabulous seasons.

Strong, with amazing pace off the mark, agile, two footed, good in the air - he was comfortable in all positions across the forward lines.

In the 1950's Finney was Preston North End - the year after he retired in 1961 the club was relegated from Division one and has never returned.

Perhaps Matt Busby was absolutely right.

A selection of facts and figures from Tom Finney's career:

- **Finney appeared in 433 Football League games for P.N.E. between 1946 and 1960.**
- **Finney scored 187 League goals at an average of a goal every 2.31 games.**
- **Finney won a First Division Runners Up medal in both 1952-53 and 1957-58 and a Second Division Championship medal in 1950-51.**
- **Finney made a full League debut versus Leeds on the opening day of the 1946-47 season and his farewell against Luton on the final day of the 1959-60 season.**
- **Finney reached double figures for goals in 10 of his 14 seasons with P.N.E. He never scored a League or Cup hat-trick but scored 4 goals for England vs. Portugal.**
- **Finney appeared in 40 F.A. Cup ties, including the 1954 Final, scoring 23 goals.**
- **Finney won 76 England Caps in the first 101 Internationals following the Second World War. He played against 23 different countries and finished on the losing side only a dozen times.**
- **Finney played for his country in three different positions, scoring 30 times. He played 21 times with Stanley Matthews in the side.**
- **Finney played 17 times for the Football League Representative XI and appeared in 2 World Cup ties.**